Theresa Nelson

DEVIL
STORM

DEVIL STORM

STORM

Theresa Nelson

AN AUTHORS GUILD BACKINPRINT.COM EDITION

Devil Storm

AN AUTHORS GUILD BACKINPRINT.COM EDITION

Published by iUniverse.com, Inc.

For information address:
iUniverse.com, Inc.
620 North 48th Street, Suite 201
Lincoln, NE 68504-3467
www.iuniverse.com

Originally published by Orchard Books

ISBN: 0-595-14413-6

Printed in the United States of America

• For my mother,
ALICE CARROLL HUNTER NELSON

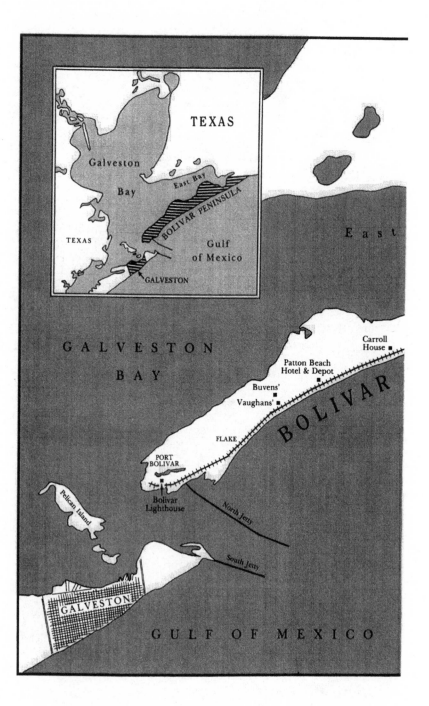

TEXAS

Galveston

Bay

East Bay

TEXAS

BOLIVAR PENINSULA

Gulf
of Mexico

GALVESTON

GALVESTON

BAY

East

Carroll
House

Patton Beach
Hotel & Depot

Buvens'

Vaughans'

BOLIVAR

FLAKE

PORT
BOLIVAR

Bolivar
Lighthouse

North Jetty

Pelican Island

South Jetty

GALVESTON

GULF OF MEXICO

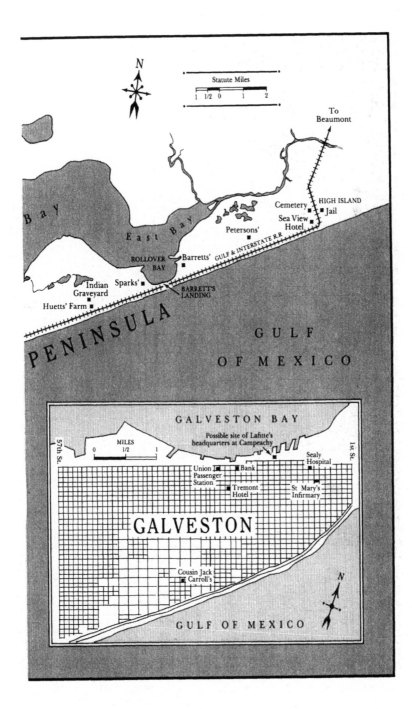

• July 1900

A lopsided moon shone over the Gulf the night old Tom came back to Bolivar. An old, gray man he was, the color of the sea on a cloudy day—clothes and skin and whiskers all gray, weather-beaten, like a ramshackle house with the paint peeled off.

He walked slowly along the beach, carrying a bent shovel over his shoulder, dragging a dirty gunnysack behind him. He paused occasionally to gaze far out on the moon-bright water as if waiting, listening. . . .

He had been here before—twenty times, thirty, maybe more; the days and months and years all ran together, until there was no figuring. Everybody up and down the peninsula had heard tell of Tom; wherever he went, the talk would follow:

"Yonder comes that old tramp," someone would say, and mothers would hustle their babies off the beach, out of harm's way.

"I s'pose you heard he eats dogs—hypnotizes 'em some way, then knocks 'em over the head. . . ."

"I wouldn't put it past the old devil. . . ."

"They say he has fits. . . ."

"Likely on account of his blood being mixed—good Lord never intended such a thing. You know his mama was one of them cannibal Indians used to live around here, and his father was black as they come. . . ."

"Naw, you got that backwards. His mama was a slave girl straight off the boat, and it's well known that he claims his papa was old Lafitte himself. . . ."

"No!"

"Not the pirate!"

"Well, why else you think he carries that old shovel around with him?"

"I thought it was for hittin' dogs on the head. . . ."

"Shoot, no—he's got to have it case he ever comes across his papa's treasure. Didn't you ever hear that?"

"Well, I don't believe a word of it myself, but there's those that do. . . ."

Every now and again he'd bend down and pick up something out of a tide pool—a sand dollar, or a seashell, or a piece of driftwood—poke it into the sack, and walk on again, muttering softly to himself. After a while he stopped between two sand hills, made a little pile of dried salt grass and driftwood, and lit it with an old sulfur match he pulled from a ragged pocket. The fire flickered unevenly, then settled into a fair blaze, fair enough to cook the pair of fat little croakers he slapped in a beat-up pan over it.

Off down the beach another light blinked steadily, on again, off again, on again, off again. . . . *That'll be the lighthouse down at Port Bolivar,* the old man told himself. He knew everything there was to know about this skinny strip of marshland that lay like a three-humped camel between the Gulf of Mexico and Galveston's East Bay. He knew its every twist and bulge; he knew the particular feel of the sand under his feet and the certain taste of the salt air on his tongue; he knew the winds before they blew, the waves before they broke, and all the creatures that swam or crawled or cried in the night. He knew everything.

And now he had come back.

BOOK ONE

That which hath been is now;
and that which is to be hath already been;
and God requireth that which is past.

—ECCLESIASTES, *3:15*

• Chapter 1

Walter Carroll wiped the sweat off his freckled fore-head and squinted into the setting sun. Lord, but he was sick to death of watermelons. All the hot afternoon he had wrestled with the fat green monsters, hauling them up off the vines and loading them onto the old wagon until his thirteen-year-old back ached mightily, his neck and shoulders throbbed with fatigue.

"You all right, son?" Walter's father, Richard Carroll, straightened up and looked over at the boy from across the wagon. "We've been at it a long time."

Walter managed a grin. "Yes, sir, I'm all right." He was proud to be considered man enough to work side by side with his father. Still, it was good to see the sun finally slanting off to the west in long streaks of purple and gold; Walter had begun to think it had somehow got stuck directly over his head.

Dowling, the old mule, flicked his ears back and snorted impatiently.

"Hold on there, Dowling," Mr. Carroll said soothingly. "Another half hour won't kill you." He smiled at his son. "We got a mighty good haul here, Walter. I'll warrant there's not a one of these melons under twenty pounds—ought to fetch top dollar in Galveston tomorrow."

"Yes, sir." A whisper of a breeze touched the back of Walter's neck and ruffled his hair. He looked behind him to see if the waves were picking up out in the Gulf. No. The water was flat as a pancake and deep, deep blue, without a speck of white showing anywhere, save for the line of gentle breakers at its edge. The beach looked wet —dun-colored at first, creamier where it spread out and was outlined by the black of the railroad tracks that ran parallel to the surf. Then came a swelling of grass-topped sand hills and a stretch of tangled, overgrown green that ended abruptly in a tidy little kitchen garden; between that and the brown-and-green-striped melon fields stood the gray barn and, finally, flanked by Lillie Carroll's hand-planted palm trees, the Carroll house itself, its white paint dazzling in the last strong rays of sunlight.

That white paint had been a bone of everlasting contention between Walter's mother and father. "White's not practical on the seashore," Mr. Carroll had objected. "It'll be dingy and sandblasted in a year's time. What about a pretty pink?" He was partial to pink, and some of the most fashionable houses in Galveston were pink.

"I'll not have a house that's painted like some tawdry woman," Mrs. Carroll declared. "White's a civilized color."

"Not a color atall," her husband mumbled, but he had bought the white paint. . . .

Seagulls soared high overhead. Their cries filled the air like rude laughter.

Go on, laugh. Walter sighed, turning back to the never-ending melons. *See if I care.*

For as long as he could remember, Walter had lived in the white house on the beach. His father had built it when Walter was a baby—built it with his own hands out of heart pine and Florida cypress, close enough to the water to catch the Gulf breeze, high off the ground on wooden blocks to keep it safe from storm tides. It was a fine, strong house—"shipshape," Richard Carroll called it. He had once been a ship's carpenter, and though he gave up his travels and turned farmer when he married, he had never quite got the salt water out of his veins. The very lumber he used for the house had come from the sea. He had loaded it on a schooner in Pensacola, sailed with it to Bolivar, and unloaded it in the Gulf, where it had washed ashore with the tide. Sometimes, when Walter lay in bed at night, with the sound of the waves and the wind singing in his ears, he could almost believe that the house was a mighty ship, afloat on the sea, and that when he awoke he might be anywhere in the world—anywhere at all. His head was full of odd ideas—dreams and notions that grew as fast and thick as the weeds in his father's melon fields. "Comes of having cat's eyes," his mother would say, shaking her head. Walter's eyes were hazel, flecked with green.

"*Aieeeeee!*"

"Lordamercy . . ." The war whoop was so bloodcurdling that Walter nearly jumped out of his skin. He whirled around and saw his sister Alice, younger than he was by three and a half years, standing just behind the wagon, giggling. She was a blond-headed, bony little thing, all angles and elbows, with bright brown eyes. On her left hip she was balancing a pretty baby, little Emily, the youngest of the Carroll children, who crowed and clapped her hands just as if she knew what the joke was all about.

"Shame on you, daughter! What're you doin' sneaking up on us like that? You want to give your brother heart failure?" Their father's face was stern, but his eyes twinkled. He was that soft when it came to his girls, and everybody knew it.

"Shoot, she didn't scare me," Walter scowled.

"Yes, I did too," Alice laughed exultantly. "You jumped higher'n a frog; I saw you with my own two eyes! Me and Emily's been practicing our Indian walk. Aren't we gettin' good, Papa?"

"Too good if you ask me, Miss Alice Carroll. Young ladies ought not to be spending all their time carrying on so."

Little Emily squirmed in Alice's grip and held out two chubby arms to her father. He laughed, picked her up, and swung her high over his head. "My baby girl's a papoose, is she?" Emily squealed with delight and wanted more, but he handed her back to Alice. "I got no time to play now. You take her on back to the house, daughter."

"You all close to bein' done? Mama wants to know can she put her biscuits in yet."

"You tell your mother to give us another, say, ten minutes, and we'll be right along."

"I expect that means twenty," Alice whispered to Walter, who knew it did but paid her no mind. He walked deliberately back to the fattest melon he could find and began twisting it off the vine.

Alice followed. "Need some help?"

"Girls ain't strong enough for this kind of work."

"I'm plenty strong. I bet this baby weighs more than any of these old melons!"

"Well, you ought not to carry her around all the time, then. How's she ever gonna learn to walk, anyway, with you and Papa spoilin' her rotten—that's what I'd like to know."

"Aw, Walter's still mad 'cause we scared him. Poor Walter, we got to cheer him up. Do your Indian noise, Emily—you 'member how I showed you?"

Alice beat the flat of her hand against her rounded lips, and sure enough, little Emily followed suit. "Woo, woo, woo!"

Walter tried to ignore them, but the two of them were so silly-looking standing there hooting like a pair of owls that he couldn't keep his mouth straight.

"Oh, he's grinnin' now—Walter's grinnin'!" Alice cried, dancing Emily around their brother.

"Alice, didn't I tell you to go on back to the house?" Mr. Carroll called from the other side of the wagon.

"Yes, sir, I'm goin'." Alice turned and headed across the field, but before she had gone ten yards, she wheeled about and came running back to Walter.

"I know a secret!" She fairly flung the words at him and was off again like a shot, Emily bouncing on her bony hip.

Walter sighed and shook his head. *Sisters!* Lord, they were enough to drive a fellow to distraction.

He had had a brother once. A little old curly-head named William . . .

A mosquito landed on Walter's arm and went to work. Walter held still for a minute and watched with a kind of fascination as it sucked away, filling its ugly belly with his blood. . . .

If William had lived, he'd have been seven years old come November. But he'd been stricken with the summer sickness a year ago, just a month before Emily was born.

The mosquito started to pull away, wobbling drunkenly. Walter smashed it. "Serves you right," he muttered, wiping the red streaks off on his britches.

"All right, son, that just about does it. Let's take 'er in," his father said. "You tend to the milking; I'll see to the mule and the melons."

"Yes, sir," said Walter. His stomach growled. Lord, but he was hungry.

"FOR WHAT we are about to receive, may the Lord make us truly thankful." Mr. Carroll's voice was low, his head bowed.

"Amen," said the others, except for Emily, who laughed and banged her spoon on the table and dropped a mangled crust of bread on the floor. Crockett, the squat brown dog who was hiding hopefully under the table near the baby's high chair, obligingly cleaned it up.

"Dog!" said Emily, smiling at him. It was her one word.

"Mercy, is that old dog in the house again?" Lillie Carroll scolded. "Walter, you take him outside this minute. We'll have fleas from here to December!"

"Yes'm," Walter said. "C'mon, boy. . . ."

For a while after that no one spoke. The room was full of good smells and homey, comfortable sounds—the scraping and clanking of silverware against china as fried ham, lima beans, sliced tomatoes, and buttered biscuits disappeared in short order; the baby's low gurgling and babbling; the murmur that was the sound of the sea through the open window. . . .

Walter loved that sound best of all—not that he usually noticed it much, any more than most people notice air. For that was what it was like for him—as constant and essential as the air he breathed. Once, when he was eight years old, he had gone with his mother to visit relatives in the town of Devine, just outside of San Antonio. They had stayed for a week, and everything had been very pleasant—"divine Devine," Uncle Jim had joked—but Walter had hardly slept the whole time. He had tossed and turned in the strange bed and not known what on earth was the matter, until he got home and heard that sound—the wind and the waves and the cry of the gulls. And then he had understood what it was he had been missing. . . .

"Well, Lillie, another fine supper," her husband declared, smiling at her and helping himself to a third biscuit.

Mrs. Carroll appeared not to have heard. She was toying with the food on her plate in dainty, ladylike fashion, the fork held delicately in her left hand. She was left-handed, like Walter; otherwise, you could hardly tell they were kin. She was just a little bit of a woman, scarcely five feet from top to toe. Walter, who was threatening to be tall like his father, already had to bend down to kiss her cheek.

Papa cleared his throat. "Yes, ma'am, a mighty good supper—"

This time Mama looked up. "I'm glad you're enjoying it," she murmured, as if she were speaking to a stranger.

There was an uncomfortable silence that lasted a minute or two. Then she spoke again, and Walter jumped; the sound of her voice surprised him, somehow.

"Alice found the remains of a fairly fresh campfire about a mile down the beach today." Mama's tone was even, but her brown eyes looked troubled. "That's strange, isn't it?"

"Most likely just some of the hotel guests from down at Patton Beach," Mr. Carroll said, "horseback riding or hiking. . . ."

"Well, it makes me nervous, that's all," she went on. "I don't like the idea of strangers wandering around, with us out here in the middle of nowhere—you just never know what they might be up to. I told Alice she oughtn't to be taking unsupervised walks so far from home, and I knew you'd want to speak to her about it, too."

Mr. Carroll looked seriously at his daughter, who was intent at the moment on stabbing a slippery lima bean with the tip of her knife. "Your mother's right, Alice," he said. "A young lady can't be too careful." Walter rolled his eyes. He couldn't see that the term "lady" had much to do with Alice.

Alice looked up from her bean. "But, Papa," she protested, "a mile's not far!"

"Too far for you by yourself," he replied. "Do you hear me, Alice?" The whole family understood that tone; you might just as well butt your head up against a brick wall as fight back when he used it.

"Yes, sir," Alice answered meekly. Walter knew the

small voice was purely for show; Alice was about as meek as old Crockett—they had both been known to bite.

Still, their mother seemed reassured, and Papa steered the conversation into calmer waters—something about how this promised to be the best year ever for the farmers on the peninsula, the possibility of buying a boat sometime in the near future, the baby's newest tooth—boring, comfortable talk that hummed lazily on the outskirts of Walter's mind and left it free to wander.

Tomorrow would be a good day. He and Papa would wake up early, hitch Dowling to the loaded wagon, and ride over to Barrett's Landing on the bay at Rollover. The Barretts owned a "watermelon schooner," one of a dozen or so small boats that sailed to Galveston every day carrying produce—mostly melons—from the Bolivar farms. Once the melons were on the boats and out of the way, Walter's work load would be light. Maybe he'd do some fishing, or maybe he'd swim, or maybe just spend a couple of hours doing nothing at all. Alice would want to tag after him, of course; she always did. Well, maybe he'd let her, if he felt like it, and then again maybe he wouldn't. She was all right, for a girl, but she was just a girl, after all.

Walter's eyes moved involuntarily to the slender black ribbon around his mother's neck. He hated the sight of that ribbon, hated the very threads it was made of— black for mourning, black for William. Walter gritted his teeth and looked away. Through the window he could see the blue glimmer of the Gulf.

For months he had dreamed of doing something so grand and good that Mama would forget to be sad, and everything would be the way it was before. But he hadn't for the life of him been able to think of any way to help. And then, by some perverse stroke of luck, just when he most yearned to be strong and wise and wonderful, he had turned thirteen instead. Overnight, it seemed, his feet and hands grew unconscionably big, all out of proportion to everything else. Alice said it looked like he'd grown a pair of canoes with paddles to match. His neck stretched out to expose a ridiculous-looking Adam's apple, and his voice squeaked and his sweat stank and he cut a whole new set of molars, which he needed about as much as a dog needs an extra tail—"wisdom teeth," his father called them. "Well, I'll declare, I never heard of anybody getting them so early!" But Walter reckoned they weren't anything to be proud of. He was just an honest-to-goodness freak, that was all—Mother Nature's idea of a really good joke.

It made him feel lonesome, somehow, and restless. Some mornings he would wake up and want to smash things. He would run down the beach instead, as far and fast as his legs would carry him, or stand facing the water with his hands cupped around his mouth and holler till he was hoarse, or torment Alice by tickling the soles of her feet. She cussed him for this, but it did his heart unspeakable good.

Other mornings he could scarcely lift his head from the pillow. A great weight of sadness would fall on him from out of the clear, blue sky and hold him prisoner for hours. Then, as suddenly as it had come, it was gone, leaving him to laugh and shout and run again. . . .

Walter felt Alice's eyes on him and looked up. She smiled a maddening, mysterious smile that reminded him she hadn't told him her secret yet. *For crying out loud!* He'd figured that bit about the campfire was it, and it probably was. Now she'd gone and puzzled out something else to aggravate him with. Well, if she thought he was going to pleasure her by begging to know what this deep, dark secret was, she had another think coming!

• Chapter 2

Daylight lingered well past eight of a summer evening, but Walter was too tired to linger with it. As soon as supper was over, he kissed his mother good night and dragged his weary bones out to the sleeping porch, which served as bedroom for all three children in hot weather. There he tumbled into bed without casting so much as a crumb of curiosity in Alice's direction.

He could have sworn he hadn't been asleep two minutes when the whispering started.

"Walter, you awake?"

He made no answer.

"Aw, come on, Walter, I know you hear me. You got to wake up right now." She was shaking his shoulders, tickling him.

Walter sighed, turned over, and opened his eyes. There was no use in letting her carry on until she woke up the baby; there'd be no end of trouble then. "What's the matter with you, Sister? It's the middle of the night!"

"I know. It's perfect. Look at the moon."

Walter looked. There it was, shining in the window, so close, it seemed, he could have hit it with a rock. "Looks like an old bald-headed man," he muttered. "Now leave me alone. Hell's bells."

"Better not let Mama hear you cussin'," Alice said placidly. "Come on, Walter, we got to go down to the beach."

"Good Lord, Alice, you out of your mind? I'm not goin' anywhere but back to sleep."

"Well, all right, but you won't ever know what I know if you don't come."

"That's just fine with me." Walter rolled back over on his stomach and buried his head under his pillow. For a moment he could still feel Alice standing beside his bed, breathing on his back; he fully expected the pummeling to commence at any second. But it didn't. When he poked his head out a minute later, Alice was gone. He looked over at her bed. It was empty.

"Lordy," Walter said under his breath. He was wide awake now. He knew he might as well follow her and find out what she had on her mind, or he'd never hear the end of it.

Soundlessly he pulled on his britches and crept through the house and out into the night. Up ahead he could see Alice's cotton nightgown fluttering like a white moth in the freshening wind. A small, dark form trotted along at her heels. *That'll be Crockett*, Walter told himself. He followed the two of them down the sandy path that cut through the marsh, thick with the sharp smell of salt grass and wildflowers.

They stopped on top of a little sand hill, looked back and saw him following, and waited there for him.

"I knew you'd come," Alice said as he climbed up. Crockett's tail wagged in greeting.

"Well, all right, I'm here," Walter panted. "Now, what's so dad-blamed important?"

"Just look. 'Dy'ever see anything so pretty?" Alice pointed to the moon, shining down on the Gulf like God's own glory. And in the water below another million trillion moons were shining, shimmering over and over in a radiant path that stretched from the horizon all the way back to the beach, where it broke apart and glittered like glass beads on the wet sand.

Walter shivered. Not that he was cold; it was just that the sight of that bright water gave him gooseflesh somehow, right between his shoulder blades. "Lordy," he breathed. He was suddenly glad he had come.

Alice looked at him and smiled. Two more tiny moons shone in her eyes. "Let's go down to the water," she said, and then she bunched up her nightgown around her skinny thighs and ran down the hill, over the railroad tracks, and across the beach, until she was standing knee-deep in liquid moonlight. Crockett bounded after her.

"It's a moonwater trail!" she called to Walter over the noise of the surf. "Magic! I read about it in Mama's fairy book 'safternoon."

"You're out of your mind!" Walter called back, but he followed his sister. His brains felt addled with moonlight. The wind was fresh in his face. He had pushed his britches up over his knees, and the sea was cool on his bare legs.

"No, really," Alice went on, "it's the truth! Nothin's more magical than moonwater. The moon sees everything there is to see, knows everything there is to know;

then it pours all its magic into the water. I'm tellin' you, I read the whole thing in that book. All we got to do is drink a little, and we can read minds!"

"Drink it? Drink this old salt water? Why, we'd be sick as dogs!" Walter laughed suddenly and whirled around, sending a shower of glittering drops flying from his fingertips.

"We won't, either," Alice insisted. "We don't have to drink all that much—just enough to give us the power."

"Aw, Sister, that book never meant moonwater out of the Gulf of Mexico! Lordy, I read all them stories when I was little. You got to have enchanted lakes or fairy pools or some such. . . . Anyhow, you don't really believe in all that foolishness—"

"Maybe I do and maybe I don't. Cain't hurt to try."

Walter stopped whirling and looked sternly at his sister. "This your big secret? This why you woke me up and dragged me out here in the middle of the night?"

Alice nodded slowly. "Well, you never can tell. . . ."

For a moment Walter thought about getting good and mad, but just then a fair-sized wave came tumbling in and knocked the two of them off their feet. They came up spluttering, giggling as they watched Crockett paddle back to shore and shake himself violently, then trot off into the darkness.

"Got more sense than we do," Walter choked. "I b'lieve I just swallowed some moonwater."

"Me too," Alice laughed, and then, since they were both wet to the skin anyway, they splashed around and splattered each other, shouting out loud.

"Uh-oh," Walter groaned, standing up and shaking the water off just as Crockett had done. "What's Mama gonna say 'bout your nightgown?" He didn't worry so much about his britches, which he knew would be sun-baked on his body before the morning was half gone.

"Aw, it's all right. I can hide it under my bed and put on my old one. I have to help with the washing tomorrow anyhow."

But the thought of their mother worried Walter. He dragged his sister to her feet. "Come on, Alice. We got to go on back. You know we'd catch it if they was to wake up and look for us."

"Awww . . ."

She knew it was no use arguing. Walter could be just as stubborn as old Dowling if he'd a mind to. The two of them walked ashore, splashing silver with every step.

"Hey, Walter—"

"What?"

"I'm readin' your mind."

"You're not, either—what'm I thinkin'?"

"I'll never tell," Alice giggled, and she was off in a soggy streak.

"Hell's bells!" Walter shouted, chasing after her. And then he almost had her—but not quite. She was fast for such a little squirt of a girl. He caught the dripping tail of her nightgown, but she got away. Then he grabbed her again by one of her slippery arms, and they were laughing and struggling.

All of a sudden Walter stopped laughing. He tightened his hold on Alice's arm.

"Ow! That hurts, Walter. You're hurtin' me!"

"Shh!"

"What is it?"

"I said hush!"

Walter meant it. Alice hushed.

"Look over there," he whispered, jerking his head to the left.

Alice looked. Down the beach a little way, nestled close to the sand hills, a small red campfire was burning.

• Chapter 3

The cow's name was Jane Long. "In honor of the Mother of Texas," Papa had announced the day he brought her home.

Mama was skeptical. "I don't know that the Mother of Texas would consider it such a great honor to have an old cow named after her."

"I don't see why not," Papa answered. "So long as it's a good cow."

That had settled that, and in the course of time the Carrolls had found themselves possessed of a whole slew of Texas heroes: the mule, Dick Dowling, the dog, Davy Crockett, and the old rooster, Sam Houston.

"Hey, Miz Long, come on, girl!" Walter leaned on the gate of the cow pasture, rubbing the sleep out of his eyes. It was a fine morning. The wind off the ruffled water was fresh and cool, the sun bright but not too hot just yet. Little yellow butterflies darted in and out among the orange blossoms of the trumpet vine that climbed helter-skelter on the fence. The whole world was so solid and sweet-smelling and reassuring that Walter almost laughed when he thought how different everything had seemed last night in the moonlight. Why, he and Alice had turned tail and run like the dickens at the sight of that little old campfire down the beach.

"Musta been the moonwater," he told Jane Long as he milked her. "Had us crazed. Why, my heart was poundin' so hard after I got back to bed—thought I never would drop off again."

"Walter! Hey, Walter!"

It was Alice. A sack of chicken feed was slung over her shoulder; Sam Houston, the rooster, was strutting after her, gobbling up everything she flung to him. He was Alice's particular pet, allowed out of the chicken coop on special occasions.

"I'm right over here, Sister."

"Walter, you seen Crockett? I put his breakfast in the barn, but I cain't find him anywhere."

"Aw, he's prob'ly around somewhere, chasin' nutrea rats or some such. Just leave it in there. He'll get it later on. Ow! Hell's bells, Alice, don't drop that feed over here. Your stupid chicken just pecked my foot!"

"He's not either stupid. He pecked it on purpose 'cause you always call him names."

"Aw, for cryin' out loud . . ."

"You 'bout done, Walter?" Papa called from the gate. "We ought to be gettin' along." He already had Dowling hitched to the wagon, which was groaning under the pile of fine, fat melons. "I don't know that the Barretts expect us this morning—wouldn't want them shoving off 'fore we get there."

"Yes, sir—" Walter squirted one last stream of the warm milk into the already heavy pail, then aimed another at Sam Houston's rear end. The rooster flapped his wings and squawked indignantly. Alice glowered. Walter laughed. "I'm comin' right now!" he shouted.

They breakfasted on Mama's cornbread and mayhaw jelly as they walked along beside the wagon on the rough shell road; Papa allowed that Dowling had plenty to carry without the two of them adding their well-fed carcasses to his load.

"Wouldn't be surprised if we got some rain later on today," Mr. Carroll said when they had walked for a while in companionable silence.

Walter looked up at the sky. It was serenely blue, flecked with a few wispy clouds way up high. "How can you tell?" he asked.

His father chuckled. "Old sailor's saw—'Red sky at night, sailors delight; red sky at morning, sailors take warning.' Today we had the prettiest red sunrise I ever did see. I expect you were too sleepy to notice."

Walter blushed guiltily. He'd had a deuce of a time waking up so soon after he had finally managed to get back to sleep. He looked sideways at his father, but Papa's face gave no clue to what he was thinking.

More silence, broken only by the creaking of the wagon and the clumping of Dowling's hooves.

"I just might take a look at that middle-sized tub the Barretts aren't using anymore," Papa said after a little. "Old Man Barrett says he may be thinking of letting her go if he can get a fair price."

"Well, that'd be fine," said Walter. Inwardly he sighed. Papa was always talking about buying a boat. The watermelon schooners charged a pretty penny for their services, and Walter knew his father longed for the day when he wouldn't have to depend on the likes of the Barretts to haul his melons to market. But somehow there never seemed to be any extra money.

"Couple more hauls as good as this one, we just might see our way clear . . ." His father's voice trailed off.

"Yes, sir," said Walter.

There was a sudden rustling and commotion in the tall marsh grass beside the road, and a long-legged crane took off skyward, frantically beating its wide, white wings. Dowling shied. Papa soothed him and stopped to watch the bird's awkward flapping smooth into graceful flight.

"Whoa, boy, no sense in you takin' on like some kind of racehorse. Now isn't that a pretty thing? Must've been hiding right there for the last five minutes with its heart all aquiver, waiting for us to pass, and then at just about the worst possible moment it couldn't stand it any longer." Papa scratched his chin. "You know, there's those as say a crane's an omen, but I'll be dogged if I can remember if it's supposed to be good or bad. You ever hear that, Walter?"

"No, sir."

"Well, I believe it's good. Remind me to ask your mother; she's the one would know."

"Yes, sir." Mama had a head for that sort of thing—omens and good luck charms and what a dream signified and so forth. She had learned it all as a child, from her old nurse. That day last summer when William died she had seen a little mourning dove sitting at his window, and she'd known right then what was going to happen. . . .

The crane was just a white speck now, flying westward in the blue sky.

"Giddup, Dowling," his father said. "C'mon, y'ole mule!"

THERE WERE several other melon farmers at the Rollover Landing when the Carrolls arrived with their load—Rupert Bland and Frank Buvens and Ernest Atkins with his grown boy, Earl. Loud hoots of laughter issued from the knot they formed around Lester Barrett, who was evidently entertaining them with one of his whoppers. Lester, in his mid-twenties, was the youngest and most popular of the four Barrett brothers. Everybody liked Lester. He was famous for his arm-wrestling, his sailing, his fishing, and his lies—bald-faced lies, most of them, but nobody really cared; things were always livelier when Lester was around.

Walter thought he had hung the moon and then some. It was true that Lester never missed an opportunity to rag him about his sweetheart—or want of one; he had called Walter "Romeo" ever since the day in church when he'd spied him gazing admiringly at Fanny Kate Vaughan (who just happened to be the prettiest girl in two counties, maybe more). It was also true that Lester owned the biggest, ugliest, orneriest dog on the entire peninsula—Samson, he called him. Old Samson was so mean that Lester had to chain him to keep him from eating his own kin, they said. But Walter couldn't help admiring Lester for his arrogant good looks and swaggering self-confidence, both of which he knew he sorely lacked. Besides, one day Lester had taken him around to the back of the boat shed and treated him to five puffs off his cigar. Walter felt flattered as all get-out, though he was giddy and green for hours afterward. "Hmmph,"

Alice had sniffed, when Walter had bragged to her about it, "Lester Barrett's nothin' but a show-off." Which just went to show, Walter concluded, that certain things were beyond female comprehension.

"Hey, Richard! Come on over here!" Frank Buvens called, as Walter and his father approached the landing. "Y'all hear the news?"

Mr. Carroll shook his head. "What news, Frank?" Walter's ears perked up. News was a rare and valuable commodity on Bolivar Peninsula.

"Looks like that crazy old colored tramp's come back. Lester caught him hangin' 'round the Peterson place t'other day—"

Mr. Carroll squinted. "You don't mean old Tom?"

"That's the one." Frank Buvens nodded.

The hair at the back of Walter's neck prickled. Old Tom. Tom the Tramp. The stories they whispered about him would make your blood run cold, your hair curl and turn gray—maybe even fall out if you were the nervous type.

"You sure it was Tom?" his father asked. "I'da figured him to be long dead by now."

"It was Tom, all right—Lester saw him with his own eyes, didn't you, Lester?"

"Sure did," Lester said, looking up and winking at Walter. "You better watch out, Romeo. He looked mighty hungry to me."

The men laughed, but Walter swallowed hard. He could still see that solitary campfire burning. . . . Snatches of old gossip floated up from the murky bottom of his memory—half-forgotten scraps of sweltering Sundays in the parlor with neighbors come to call and good clothes that itched and, what with the business of children being seen and not heard, nothing to do but sweat and listen. . . .

Ought to be locked up, that's what. . . .

They say he has fits. . . .

Claims his papa was old Lafitte himself. . . .

Walter had seen him once, from a distance, walking down the beach just after sunset. His cheeks burned now to think how he had cried and hidden his face in Mama's skirts, but then he had been only six or seven years old, and it was whispered that Tom could turn the Evil Eye on you if he chose. Any Bolivar child would just as soon meet the devil after dark as cross old Tom's path even in broad daylight.

Lester was warming to his tale. ". . . and then I says to him, 'Why, Tom, seeing as how he was your daddy, seems like the least he coulda done was left you a map!' "

" 'Well, suh, he did, Mistah Lestah, but I done lost it.' "

More laughter at this.

" 'Lost it!' says I. 'Why, Tom, that was a fool thing to do. What was on that map, anyhow?' "

Lester cocked his head in a comical manner, and rolled his pale blue eyes.

" 'I's afeard I disremembah, Mistah Lestah—but if you wants to give old Tom another little taste outen that bottle, it just might come to me!' "

Ernest Atkins about choked on his chewing tobacco, he laughed so hard at that.

"And then what'd you say, Lester?" asked Frank Buvens, who never could see when a joke was over.

Lester winked at him. "I said, 'Naw, Tom, I couldn't

do that—you know that whiskey'll kill a man sure as shootin'! I don't want the W.T.U. accusing me of corrupting our dark-skinned brethren, now, do I?' "

All of the men laughed louder than ever at this—all but Frank Buvens, who looked mortified; his wife was president of the Bolivar chapter of the Women's Temperance Union.

"So old Tom's come back, has he?" Walter's father said quietly.

"Looks that way," Rupert Bland answered as the men began loading melons into the Barretts' boat. He lowered his voice. "Lester is inclined to make light of the situation, and I'll swear he can make a fella laugh, all right. But just between you and me, Richard, if that nigger tramp comes sniffin' 'round my property, he's liable to find hisself more trouble than treasure."

Mr. Carroll reached back and scratched the nape of his neck meditatively. "Well, now, Rupert, seems to me Tom's nothing but a harmless old man with a cracked brain. Folks ought to just let him be, that's what I say."

"Hmmph." Rupert Bland snorted and spewed a stream of brown tobacco juice into the muddy water dockside. "You can say harmless till the cows come home—I wouldn't trust him fu'ther than I could spit."

Walter felt cold all over in spite of the heat.

I s'pose you heard he eats dogs . . .

. . . mama was one of them cannibal Indians . . .

. . . don't believe a word of it myself, but there's those that do . . . those that do . . . those that do . . .

• Chapter 4

Before midmorning, great billows of gray were crowding all the blue out of the sky. The first raindrops spattered against the Carrolls' faces as they rattled homeward in the empty wagon.

"What'd I tell you?" Papa said, pointing at the clouds. "Red sky at morning . . ."

"Yes, sir." Walter nodded absently. "Papa—"

"What is it, son?"

"You s'pose old Tom might really be Lafitte's boy?"

His father shook his head. "Let it be, Walter; let it be. No sense worrying ourselves with things as don't concern us."

"But if he's dangerous, shouldn't that concern us?"

Papa spat. "Shoot, boy, old Tom's been showing up on these beaches for as long as I can remember—probably for a lot longer than that; old-timers say he's been coming 'round for nigh onto forty years, off and on. But I never heard of him doing anybody any harm. People just like to hear themselves talk, that's all. I'm telling you, just let it be." Papa stared off into space for a minute. Then he spoke again, a little more gruffly. "And there's to be no mention of this at home, either. I won't have your mother all upset over nothing, you hear me . . . ?"

RAIN WAS coming down in torrents by the time the family sat down to the noonday meal. Little Emily was cutting a new tooth and was fractious. Mama wasn't much better; storms always set her teeth on edge.

"Sit up straight, Walter; I do hate to see you slouch so. I wish you could have seen my father. He was a Confederate officer, you know. Never would have caught him slouching."

"Yes, ma'am," Walter sighed, doing his best to oblige.

"Alice, don't play with your food. You're too big a girl for that kind of foolishness."

"Yes, ma'am."

Lightning flashed in jagged streaks out over the Gulf. Thunder boomed like the voice of God.

Their mother shuddered. "Goodness, I'm nervous as a cat. . . ."

"No need to worry, sweetheart," Papa reassured her. "This storm will blow itself out in no time. Besides, you know we're perfectly safe in this house."

Lillie fingered the black ribbon at her throat. "That's what you always say."

"That's because it's the truth, Lillie." Papa's voice was patient, but it sounded tired around the edges—disappointed, Walter thought.

"I like storms," said Alice, slipping into her father's lap and winding her arms around his neck.

"I know, Punkin," he answered gently. Mama looked

away, but Walter caught a glimpse of her eyes. They were red and watery.

Thunder rumbled again. The house shook with it. Little Emily began to whimper.

"Come on, baby," Mama said, picking her up and carrying her off to the rocking chair. "Don't be afraid. . . ."

Walter put down his fork. He wasn't hungry anymore.

As soon as the dinner things were cleared away, he ran out through the rain to the barn and climbed up to the hayloft. It was the best place in the world during a storm. Besides, he had to get out of the house for a while, away from whatever it was that was wrong with his parents. It was as if some invisible thing would spring up between them sometimes, something that sucked up all the air in the house until there was none left for anybody else to breathe.

Walter shook the water from his hair and clothes and flopped down in the warm straw. The knots in his stomach began to come loose. The rain drummed steadily on the tin roof. Down below, Jane Long was standing in her stall like the smart cow she was. Dowling, on the other hand, might stay out in the rain for days on end and never fathom why he was getting so wet. He was dumb, even for a mule.

Where did old Tom go when it rained? Walter wondered. The thought of the tramp gave him a creepy feeling up his spine that wasn't really all that unpleasant now that he was safe in the hayloft. Nothing much ever happened in Bolivar; a little mystery was exciting, made his blood race, like the coming of a storm. Walter lay on his back and stared up at the underside of the roof.

Pirates and slave girls and cannibal Indians danced before his eyes—why, that old man was just chock-full of possibilities! Never mind that Papa had insisted he was harmless; Papa had been known to be wrong on occasion. . . .

And what of the treasure? Mightn't there really be a treasure, after all? It was a well-known fact that old Lafitte had been as rich as Croesus—richer, most likely, what with all the gold he stole on the high seas, not to mention the dirty profits he piled up in the slave trade. Rumor had it he'd buried the lot when he got wind of the news that the U.S. government was going to run him off Galveston Island—buried it the Lord only knew where, then set his base afire and sailed away forever. Nobody could say for sure what happened to him, but it was assumed he died the bloody pirate's death that he deserved and never got around to digging up all that lovely treasure—which meant that it was still out there somewhere, just waiting to be found. . . .

Every now and again *The Galveston Daily News* would run an article on somebody with second sight who had unearthed a handful of old coins or a rusty trinket or two, and then for a while the price of divining rods would run sky-high, and an epidemic of treasure-hunting fever would rage. Nothing ever came of it.

But who's to say nothing ever will? Walter asked himself as he lay dreaming in the straw, while the lightning flashed and the thunder crackled and the rain poured just out of reach. *Why, anybody might find that old treasure one day—well, sure, why not? Anything's possible. . . .*

"Walter! Walter, you up there?" Alice's shrill voice

cut through Walter's wonderings just as slick as a knife through butter. "Walter!"

For crying out loud! Not a moment's peace! "Here I am, Alice—you don't have to yell so!"

Alice scrambled up the ladder to the loft and knelt down beside her brother. She was out of breath and wet all over. Her eyes were glittery bright. "I figured you'd be out here. Everybody else is takin' naps." She made a wry face. "But I couldn't sleep. You wanta tell ghost stories?"

"Maybe," said Walter. He sat up, smiling dangerously. "Maybe I got somethin' better than ghost stories— somethin' *true* . . . but I prob'ly shouldn't tell you."

"Why not?"

" 'Cause it's liable to scare the daylights out of you, that's why not."

"Come on, Walter, tell!" Alice begged.

Walter shrugged, picked up a straw and started twirling it between his fingers. "Well, don't say I didn't warn you," he began, lowering his voice. "Old Tom's back!"

Alice's mouth dropped open. "No!" she breathed, her eyes wide as saucers. "Tom the *Tramp*? But everybody thought he was dead!"

"Well, they thought wrong. It was all the talk down at the landing this morning. Lester Barrett says he saw him big as life."

"Lester Barrett?" Alice looked disappointed. "Aw, Walter, how you know it's true then?"

"I just know, that's all. *Think*, Sister—who do you s'pose was burnin' that campfire on the beach last night?"

Alice drew in her breath. "Not old Tom!"

Walter nodded darkly. "I'm tellin' you, it's a wonder

we weren't killed. What if Tom had thought we were spyin' on him, tryin' to steal his papa's treasure? He'da murdered us for sure!"

Alice hugged her knees against her chest. "I guess we had a mighty close call, then, didn't we?"

"Nobody ever had a closer and lived to tell it."

"My," she murmured, shivering appreciatively. "I wish I'da seen him, though. Tell about that time you seen him, Walter. Tell how he looked."

"Well, I guess he was about the ugliest thing I ever laid eyes on, that's all. There he was, walkin' down the beach, draggin' that old sack behind him. . . . You know they say he keeps dead bodies in there, case he feels the hunger comin' on him."

"Weren't you scared?"

"Naw, not all that much, 'cause I could see the blood dribblin' out the side of his mouth, so I knew he was just done eatin'. A headhunter's like a lion or a bear that way—he won't bother you if he's got a bellyful. But if you was ever to meet him when he's hungry, you got to offer him food right away or he'll gobble you up in nothin' flat."

"My," Alice said again, though she had heard it all a hundred times before. "What happened then, Walter? What'd you do then?"

"Well, I was just gettin' ready to follow him, to see if he'd lead me to his treasure, but then Mama started callin' for me to come help her with something, so I had to go. But I tell you what, next time just might be a whole different story."

Alice looked thoughtful. "Walter," she said after a moment, "why do you s'pose it's takin' old Tom so long to find that treasure anyhow? Seems like if he was really the pirate's boy, wouldn't be any trouble atall."

Walter shrugged. "Likely on account of the curse."

"What curse?"

"Why, there's *always* a curse on pirate's gold 'cause of the sinful way they get it. I never heard yet of the pirate that lived to enjoy himself for long—nor any of his family, neither." Walter's eyes shone as another thought struck him. "Course, now, if *we* were to find it, it'd be a whole nother thing; our blood's not tainted, you see, so the curse couldn't work on us."

"It couldn't?"

"Oh, no—the treasure'd be ours, free and clear. All the people it was stole from are bound to be long dead, so it's just finders, keepers now."

"And then we'd be rich, wouldn't we?"

"Well, I should say." Walter leaned back in the straw, his hands behind his head. "Richer'n anybody."

"What would you do then, Walter? What would you do if you were rich?"

Walter closed his eyes and smiled as he imagined his mother's face when she read the headline in the *News*: *BOLIVAR YOUTH FINDS LAFITTE'S FABULOUS FORTUNE—WALTER CARROLL DISCOVERS RICHES BEYOND BELIEF!* "Oh no, Walter—you didn't *really!*" she would say, and he would laugh and say oh yes, he did, and then he would reach into the golden casket—the small one with the red velvet lining that had been hidden at the very bottom of the big chest —and pull out the most precious treasure of all, a necklace made of diamonds and emeralds and rubies and pearls and, oh, any number of nice things. And he would slip it around her neck, and she would be so proud and happy that she would untie that old black ribbon once and for all and never, ever be sad anymore. . . .

"Come on, Walter, what would you do?"

"I'm thinkin', I'm thinkin'. . . ." And then he'd never have to look at another watermelon for as long as he lived. Oh no, he'd give up farming altogether and take the whole family to live in the mansion he'd buy for them in Galveston. Why, he knew the very one—grand as a castle, with balconies and towers and turrets and all. . . . And there'd be a sailing boat for Papa, and pretty play-toys for the baby, and music lessons for Alice, who would learn to be a lady and forget all her rag-tag tom-foolery. . . . And by and by he himself, Walter Carroll, Esquire, would be looking so fine and rich that Fanny Kate Vaughan was bound to pass him on the street one day and wonder who the handsome young swell might be. . . .

"Walter!"

Walter opened his eyes. They glistened in the dim light that spilled through the cracks in the wall. "Oh, I don't know, Sister. No tellin' what I'd do."

"Well, I know what I'd do," said Alice. "I'd ride the train to High Island every blessed day, and eat ice cream at the Sea View Hotel, and never do a lick of work, and give up school altogether."

"Why, then you'd be ignorant!"

"Maybe," Alice admitted, "but I'd be so rich, no-body'd care."

"I s'pose not. . . ." Walter stretched a mighty stretch and sat up. "Listen!" he said, putting his head to one side.

"What is it?"

"The rain," said Walter. "It's stopped."

It had been just a baby of a storm, after all. The sunlight was blinding when they came out of the barn, the sky blue again but for some little rags of cloud that were blowing away down the beach. Every leaf stood out sharply, greener than green, dripping brightness. An unreasoning joy sprang up in Walter's soul and bubbled over to the whole, fresh-washed world. Even Alice looked good to him. "Come on!" he shouted, and his legs began to run of their own accord. "Let's go down to the beach!"

And then for an hour there was nothing in the universe but the two of them and the sea and the sky, the blue, blue sky and the blue-green sea, great swells of it, rushing wave over wave, with the little fish called shiners flashing silver all through it, and the mullets leaping high above, and the gulls swooping low to see what the storm had churned up for their supper. And Walter swam like a great fish himself, all his awkwardness vanished as if by some magic in the water, while Alice knelt in the shallows and laughed, her knees making muddy valleys in the warm, wet sand.

OFF DOWN the beach a little way, hidden from view by the sand hills, the old man crouched in the tall grass, watching. He watched the children as a cat watches a bright object swung at the end of a string, but unlike a cat, he made no move to pounce. The children played, and he watched, and that was all. The dog, Crockett, sat beside him, shivering with pleasure as Tom scratched him slowly behind the ears.

• Chapter 5

$\mathbf{M}$r. Carroll had business to attend to in Galveston the next day. The children rode in the wagon with him down to the depot to await the arrival of the Gulf & Interstate, the two-year-old steam engine that would carry him to town. Walter had hoped to go along, as he was allowed to do every so often. Those were the finest of days, what with riding the great black train as it chugged down the peninsula, stopping to let off passengers here or pick up others there, ending up at Port Bolivar, where the railroad cars would be loaded on the barge *L. P. Featherstone* and shoved through the waters to Galveston by the tug *T. W. Terry*. And then there was the island city itself. Walter loved the noise of the wharves and the confusion of the markets—the shouting, clattering, churning wonder of it all.

Papa never wanted to dawdle and gaze, however. He seemed uncomfortable in town, out of place, even in his best clothes. He would take his son's hand—Walter's face would burn with the shame of it, big as he was, but there was no escaping that iron grip; it was as if his father thought Galveston might gobble the boy up if he gave it half a chance—and steer him through the busy streets until they reached the four-story building at Strand and Twenty-second, where Mr. Carroll did his banking. That done, father and son would ride the mule-drawn trolley as far as it went (Walter yearned after the modern electric ones, but Papa considered electricity a dangerous fad), then walk the rest of the way to the home of their Galveston relatives. Cousin Jack Carroll was a big, good-natured, red-headed fellow with a booming voice, a wife named Mary Agnes, and a whole bunch of red-headed babies that Walter couldn't for the life of him learn to tell apart; he had counted something like three sets of twins, but they were never still long enough for him to be certain. He and Papa would eat the spectacular dinner that Mary Agnes always prepared for them, spend the rest of the evening listening to Cousin Jack's interminable stories, and then go to sleep in beds vacated by assorted children, who obligingly doubled up to make room for their guests. The next day would generally be the first over again, but reversed, ending up with a late afternoon homecoming. Full to overflowing with so much excitement, Walter would sigh contentedly at the sight of the quiet fields and the white house on the beach, and vow never, ever to leave home again—until the next time he was allowed.

Today was not to be one of those times.

"I'd rather you stay here, son," Papa had told him privately. "I'd feel better knowing there was a man at home, with these wild stories about old Tom floatin' around. Not that I think there's a thing in the world to worry about," he had added quickly, seeing the look on Walter's face.

"Yes, sir," Walter had said. He could hardly help feeling flattered at being called a man, but he was sorry to miss out on the trip all the same.

"Now, Alice," Papa went on, as the wagon pulled up to the depot, "you be a good girl and help your mother." He handed the baby to her big sister. "And I'll try to bring you all something pretty from town."

"Yes, sir," said Alice, her eyes shining.

"Walter, I'd 'preciate it if you'd see to turning those new melons on that south patch. I noticed yesterday that a couple of 'em were beginning to go yellow on the bottom. And see if you can find where old Crockett's got to —he never came home all day yesterday. I don't want him worryin' Frank Buvens's cows like he did that other time."

"Yes, sir, I'll see to everything."

Their father opened his mouth to say something else, but just then the wail of a whistle split the air, and the G & I came thundering down the track. It was a splendid specimen of a train, a prince among steam engines. The children all admired it greatly. They stood as close as they dared and waved and waved as it labored to a stop under a mighty cloud of black smoke. Papa climbed aboard and waved back; he was the only passenger at the depot that morning. The engineer, whose name was Jelly Ingram, waved too, and so did three ladies in picture hats, two little boys in white sailor suits, and Mrs. Leola Sparks from down at Rollover—all on their way to Galveston for a holiday, Walter judged, except for old Mrs. Sparks, who was probably going over to Sealy Hospital or St. Mary's Infirmary to perform Good Works. Mrs. Sparks was famous for her Good Works.

"Good-bye!" Walter yelled over the clamor of the wheels and the beating of his heart as the train pulled away. "Good-bye!"

"Bye, Papa!" Alice called.

"Bye-bye," said little Emily, waving with one hand and holding on tightly to Alice with the other. "Bye-bye . . ."

And the train was gone. The steel rails sizzled where it had passed. Walter leaned over and touched one gingerly, then jerked his finger away. "Hot as fire," he murmured.

RICHARD CARROLL settled himself on the plush-covered seat and prepared to enjoy his trip. He liked trains. Boats were best, in his opinion, but trains were fine in their way, even if they were a bit lumbering, clumsy, compared to the mighty ships he had sailed.

He looked out the window at the expanse of blue water racing past. Sometimes he missed those days at sea. . . . Not that he wouldn't give it up all over again to be with his family—not that he regretted his choice; it was just that sometimes, in the last year especially, he had found himself yearning for the solitude, the peace of the open water. . . . But then he had never *really* given it up—not entirely. On a Bolivar farm there was always the sound, the smell, the everlasting presence of the sea. Lillie couldn't understand its hold on him. She was deathly afraid of water herself. Though she had married a sailor and lived by the Gulf all her adult life, she had never really got used to it—never even learned to swim.

Sometimes Richard wondered why she had ever married him at all. They came from such different worlds, he and Lillie. She was the daughter of a proud old Mississippi family that had lost everything in the war and moved to Texas when it was over. He was the son of plain folk, a gentle Quaker mother and a father who had been a seafaring man like himself. Yet Richard and his bride had been happy enough, for a time. . . . Of course, it had been hard for Lillie, learning to be a farmer's wife. She would have preferred to settle in town—Houston, maybe, where she had lived as a child, or San Antonio, near her brother—somewhere more "civilized," as she put it. But they had got on pretty well, all things considered, until William died. . . .

Just a year ago today it was. Richard took a deep breath and let it out slowly. He had tried not to think of it—hadn't even mentioned it at home this morning, in the hope that Lillie might be spared the reminder. He knew she blamed him for the child's death, though she had never said it in so many words. *And who knows?* he asked himself for the thousandth time, *Maybe she's right. . . . Maybe if we hadn't been stuck out here in the middle of nowhere, if it hadn't taken so long to get the doctor, maybe we wouldn't have lost him. Who can say?*

"Pardon me, Mr. Carroll, is this seat taken?"

Richard looked up. He had been so lost in thought that he hadn't noticed Leola Sparks approaching down the aisle on his right. "Why no, ma'am," he answered, collecting himself. "I'd be pleased to have you join me."

With a rustling of petticoats and black muslin, Mrs. Sparks deposited her stout self in the seat beside him, her kind old face glowing from the heat and exertion of

travel and . . . something else, Richard decided, judging
from a certain agitation in her manner. Leola Sparks
had something on her mind, it was plain.

"You're looking mighty well, Mrs. Sparks," he re-
marked politely.

"Why, thank you, Mr. Carroll. Though heaven knows
I'm not a one to pride myself on looks—'No fool like an
old fool,' as the saying goes. But I'm thankful to say my
health is good, which is a great blessing, of course."

"Yes, ma'am."

"And how are you and all your family?"

"We're very well, thank you."

"Well, I'm delighted to hear it. You know, I've been
so concerned about Mrs. Carroll. I do wish she'd return
to church; it would be such a comfort to her. I remember when my little daughter was taken; it like to have
killed me too. I don't believe I could have gone on without the Lord's help. . . ."

"Yes'm, I'm sure you're right," Richard said quietly.
He still found it quite impossible to talk about William.

"Perhaps next year, when the baby is a little older,"
Mrs. Sparks suggested.

"Maybe so," Richard said vaguely.

Mrs. Sparks maintained a respectful silence for a moment, then leaned toward him, as if unable to contain
herself any longer. She lowered her voice. "I s'pose you've
heard the news?"

"What news is that, Mrs. Sparks?"

"Why, old *Tom's* back, Mr. Carroll—didn't you
know?"

"Yes'm, now that you mention it, I did hear something of the sort over at the Landing yesterday morning."

Mrs. Sparks looked disappointed, but then she bright-
ened again. "Well, you don't know the half of it then,
Mr. Carroll, if you were there in the morning; it was
yesterday *afternoon* that the real to-do took place. It just
so happened that I was there for the whole thing. I was
over at Grady Barrett's, lending Mary Bell a hand with
Sister Sue—she's got the colic, you know—"

"No, ma'am, I didn't."

"Goes stiff as a board and cries for hours. I told Mary
Bell what she needs is a good dose of Mrs. Winslow's
Soothing Syrup. Which reminds me, I must try and pick
some up for her at the infirmary in Galveston—I'm on
my way over there right now, as a matter of fact. You
know, there's the awfullest influenza been striking people down left and right, and here it is the middle of
summer! I tell you, Mr. Carroll, it's enough to break
your heart. . . . But dear me, where was I?"

Richard did his best to backtrack through the barrage
of information. "A to-do at the Barretts' . . . ?"

"Oh my, yes. Well, it was all on account of this tramp
business, you see; we were all discussing it, naturally,
and Mary Bell was just remarking that there wasn't a one
of us safe in our beds these days, when there came a loud
knocking at the door. Well, it set our hearts to racing,
let me tell you, but turns out it was none other than
Sheriff D. W. Elliott himself, from over at High Island.
Said he was looking for Lester Barrett. Of course, you
know that Lester has all his meals with his brother Grady
and Mary Bell, which was why the sheriff thought he
might find him there, but wouldn't you know Lester was
gone on his boat right then and wasn't expected back for
at least another hour. But the sheriff said he just believed

he'd wait, if it wouldn't be putting anybody out, and naturally Mary Bell said why no, certainly it wouldn't— although I could see right away that she was mortified because she didn't have a thing baked that she could offer him, what with the baby being so colicky and all. But it just so happened that by the grace of Providence I had thought to bring over two of my pies—they were right outside in my buggy. I forgot to bring them in when I arrived—I'm getting absentminded as a turnip— so I fetched them, and we all had a lovely refreshment."

Mrs. Sparks paused for breath. Richard began to wonder if she would ever get to the point, or if there *was* a point. "And did Lester finally get back?" he asked, half-afraid to hear the answer.

"Oh my, yes—and Rupert Bland with him. It seems that Mr. Bland had gone along on the boat—something to do with trying to get a better price for his canta-loupes. . . . So anyhow, they all shook hands, and then right straight out Sheriff Elliott looked Lester in the eye and asked him would he be interested in a job as Bolivar deputy. Just like that! Well, everybody was mighty surprised, let me tell you—Lester Barrett most of all, from the look of him. And he told the sheriff that he was honored to be asked and all but he had never really given much thought to a career in politics, and besides, he didn't believe his family could spare him from their boat business. But Sheriff Elliott said they wouldn't have to spare him; he probably wouldn't have to do one blessed thing. It was just that he'd had several people pestering him about the tramp, and he'd feel a lot better about the situation if he had a deputy to help him keep an eye out for trouble, although he didn't really expect any. And to tell you the truth, Mr. Carroll, I'm inclined to agree with the sheriff. It's always been my feeling that old Tom is more to be pitied than anything else—'There but for the grace of God go I,' don't you know. . . . But of course, you can't be too cautious about a thing like that, especially as so many of our families have children to think of."

"Yes, ma'am," said Richard. He felt a twinge of worry but shook it off. There was nothing to worry about, he was quite sure of it. . . .

Mrs. Sparks showed no sign of letting up. "And so, as I was saying, here was the sheriff wanting to deputize young Lester, and Lester trying to make up his mind, when right out of the blue Rupert Bland says, 'Excuse me, Sheriff, but if Lester's too busy to take the job, I just might be able to see my way clear—' So naturally we could all see right off that his feelings were hurt that he hadn't been asked to begin with. But the sheriff said he really appreciated the offer and all, but it was Lester he wanted. Well, Mr. Bland didn't say a word after that, but it was plain he was just cross as two sticks. The Blands are all that way, I'm afraid. They absolutely cannot stand to have anybody else take first place. Why, I'll never forget how aggravated his father was when Tiger Terry bested him in the spelling bee at the old W.O.W. Hall. . . ."

And Mrs. Sparks was off on another track entirely. Richard waited patiently until she paused for breath again. "And so what was it Lester decided, Mrs. Sparks?"

"Oh, mercy me, didn't I tell you? Well, he finally said yes indeed, he'd be glad to be deputy if it would put the sheriff's mind at ease. So that was that. And you mark my

words, Mr. Carroll, I wouldn't be atall surprised if great
things came of this for Lester Barrett. Why, you never
know—he could very well have a future in politics after
all. There's just no telling what the Lord has in store for
any of us. . . . Why, I recall how little mind I paid it
when my dear brother Davis told me he was bringing
his new acquaintance, Mr. Wesley Sparks, to church the
next Sunday, when it just so happened I was scheduled
to sing the solo, 'Rock'd in the Cradle of the Deep.' I
remember it well. . . ."

Richard sighed inwardly as Mrs. Sparks chattered on.
It was going to be a longer trip than he had originally
anticipated.

ALICE AND EMILY stopped at the beach to hunt for sand
dollars on the way back from the depot, while Walter
took the wagon home; he fully intended to go straight
to the fields and turn melons. But then he remembered
he'd never asked his mother what kind of an omen a
crane might be, and as it seemed as good an excuse as
any to put off work a little longer, he decided to go
look for her.

She sat on the front porch, rocking.

"Mama," he began, and then he stopped. There was
something the matter with her eyes again.

"You feelin' bad?" he asked gently. It just about
killed him to see her unhappy. He loved his mother
better than anything else in the world. He couldn't
help it.

"I'm all right, son. Just a little tired, is all." She took
his hand and pressed it to her cheek. It felt wet.

"You want me to get you a drink of water?" Walter

wished to goodness he'd gone straight to turn the melons after all.

"No, thank you," she murmured. "I'm not thirsty. . . . Was there something you wanted to talk about?"

"Uh, yes'm, but—but it's not really important."

"That's all right. Go on—I'd like to hear."

Walter cleared his throat. He was feeling more and more foolish by the minute. "It's just—well, Papa told me I should ask you—whether a crane's a good omen or a bad omen. We surprised one yesterday on the way over to the Landing."

His mother was quiet for a moment. She sighed a long, shuddering sigh. "Do you remember—did it fly north or south?" she asked at last.

Walter tried to think. "Well, let's see . . . the sun hadn't been up too long; it was still behind me, I guess. . . . Well, I guess it flew sort of westerly."

Mama shook her head. "You can't tell then. North would mean bad luck, south is good, but west—well, west might mean anything, I suppose." She smiled wanly. "Not much help, am I?"

"Oh, it's no matter. It was just a silly thing, anyhow. . . ." Walter started to pull away, but his mother kept her grip on his hand.

"You know what today is, Walter?"

"No, ma'am." Somehow, Walter didn't want to know.

"It was one year ago today that your little brother died," she whispered.

Walter felt suddenly sick to his stomach. "I—I guess I forgot. . . ."

"Oh, Walter, you mustn't forget your brother!" Mama cried. "We can't ever forget William. . . ."

"No, ma'am," Walter said miserably. "I didn't mean I'd forgot *him*—"

Mama looked away. "I believe your father forgot too. He never said a word about it this morning. . . . Well, there, never mind; I s'pose that's just the way men are. . . ."

"I—I got to go now, Mama," Walter stammered. "I got to go tend to the melons." This time he managed to pull his hand free and escape, his eyes smarting. He ran around to the back of the house, stopped at the pump, and stood there jerking the handle up and down, splashing the cool water on his hot face.

"Walter, come quick!"

"Whaaa . . ." Walter was so startled that he jumped about two feet off the ground. He whirled around and glared at Alice—it was Alice, of course.

"Good Lord, Sister, how many times I got to tell you not to come sneakin' up on a person that way?"

"I'm sorry, Walter. I wasn't tryin' to scare you this time, honest. But you got to come right quick, 'fore he gets away—"

" 'Fore who gets away?"

"Tom the Tramp," said Alice breathlessly, her eyes bright as new copper pennies. "It's old Tom himself."

Walter's mouth dropped open. "What're you talkin' 'bout, Sister?"

"Old Tom—I seen him with my own two eyes. He's off down the beach a little ways! And Walter—" Alice grabbed her brother's arm and squeezed tight. "He's *diggin'*!"

Walter's heart skipped a beat. "You sure it's him?"

"Got to be—nobody else 'round here looks like that."

"What'd you do with Emily?" Walter cried, panic rising in his throat. "You didn't leave her down there!"

"Course not, silly. I gave her to Mama. And I didn't say anything, neither. Come on, Walter, don't you want to see him? He's even uglier than you said."

"Well, sure I do," said Walter, but suddenly he wasn't at all sure that this was the truth. It was all well and good to *talk* about old Tom, to lie up safe and warm in your own bed at night and get all shivery at the *thought* of him, but to actually meet him face to face—that was another thing altogether. . . .

"Well, come *on*, then," said Alice, dancing with impatience.

"I'm comin'," Walter said. He had to follow her. He couldn't let Alice see he was scared.

"Wait a minute," she said, once they had started out. "We better bring some food with us, case he's hungry. 'Member what you said 'bout headhunters—"

Hell's bells, Walter groaned inwardly. Aloud he said, "Aw, we don't need to worry with that. We prob'ly won't be gettin' close enough to feed him."

"Just in case," Alice insisted. "Cain't hurt. . . ."

The kitchen was empty. "That's good luck," she whispered. "Mama must be puttin' Emily down for a nap." She rushed about, piling a bowl high with whatever presented itself—a slice of chess pie, cornbread, mayhaw jelly, some ham, a tomato or two. "Think that oughta do it?" she asked.

"That oughta do it," he answered grimly, wishing to Christmas he were in Galveston at this very minute, listening to one of Cousin Jack's boring stories.

The trip down to the beach had never seemed so

short. Alice ran like a house afire, and Walter couldn't let her get ahead of him. . . .

"Get down," she panted, when they reached the sand hills, "else he'll see us."

They dropped to their knees, then flattened out on their bellies and slithered like snakes to the top of the nearest hill. Alice peered through the prickly salt grass and pointed just beyond the railroad tracks. "There he is, yonder," she whispered, her mouth pressed up against her brother's ear. "He looks older'n God, don't he?"

Walter's eyes followed her finger, and then he saw him too: he was old, all right, so old that Walter couldn't rightly tell what color he was. He didn't look like any white man Walter had ever seen before, but he wasn't all that black, either. . . . He was bent over his work, the shovel digging, then flying up again, showering sand. He might be old, but he looked plenty strong. Crockett was standing at his side—old Crockett, docile as a lamb, his tail wagging slowly. So that's where he'd got to. . . . Walter tried to swallow, but his spit had gone dry as a desert.

• Chapter 6

Let's go down and talk to him," Alice said suddenly.

Walter stared at her. "Good Lord, Sister, why would we want to do that?"

"Why, to find out about the treasure! We could throw him the food, to keep him friendly, and then just kinda ease up a little closer. . . ."

"For cryin' out loud, Alice, you make it sound like tamin' a jackrabbit!"

Alice looked at her brother in surprise. "You're not scared, are you, Walter?"

"Shoot, no," he muttered. "Who said anything about bein' scared?"

"Well then, let's go talk to him," said Alice. "We can always run if he gets mean. We're bound to be able to run faster than him."

"It ain't a question of who can run faster," Walter explained. "With Papa gone, you're my responsibility, and I cain't take any chances on you gettin' hurt or somethin'."

"Why, Walter Carroll, I believe you *are* scared!"

"I am not either scared."

"Y'all gonna set up there all mornin' whisperin'?"
It was the tramp. He was leaning on the handle of his
shovel, staring straight at them across the sand.

"Now you done it," Walter breathed. For a moment
he was frozen. He wanted to run, to get out of there,
but he knew that if he did, Alice would never, ever let
him forget it. He stood up tall and threw his shoulders
back.

"Mornin'," he called out, making his voice as deep
as he could.

Tom nodded. "Mornin'."

Now Alice piped up. "Whatchya diggin' for—
arsters?" Walter shot her a disbelieving look.

"Guess I got more sense than that," said Tom. "Speck
I'd go on over bayside if I's wantin' arsters. Speck I'd
try a little water, too."

"Aw, Alice was only jokin'," Walter tried. "Ever'body
knows you cain't find arsters in the sand."

Tom didn't say anything to that. He started digging
again. Walter's palms began to sweat.

"You hungry?" Alice blurted out. "We brought lots
of food." She rose and held out the bowl.

Tom stood up straight again and cocked his head
suspiciously. "You want to feed me? Why's that?"

"No reason," Walter said quickly. "We just—just
thought you might feel like eatin'—"

"And talkin'," Alice added.

"Talkin'?" Tom rubbed his gray-whiskered chin and
considered the matter for a moment or two. "Ain't nobody ever offered to feed old Tom just so's they could
hear him flap his jaw," he said at last, and he grinned

a crooked grin. He had a gold tooth right in front, on top; it glinted in the sunlight. "But I guess I ain't got no objection. What you got there?" He eyed the bowl with considerable interest.

"All kinda nice things," said Alice, darting down and handing him the food, then darting back again to Walter's side.

Tom sat in the sand and started to eat. Warily, Walter and Alice inched down the sand hill, over the tracks, and sat across from him, wide-eyed, watching his every move. . . . Walter had expected him to eat greedily, but he took his time, savoring each bite, making little clucking noises with his tongue. Every now and again he'd share a morsel or two with Crockett.

"Mighty good, mighty good," he said, once he had polished off every last crumb from the bowl and licked his fingers like a cat. "Now, what you want me to talk about?"

Walter gulped. "If you please, sir"—he wasn't sure if it was proper to address a tramp as sir, but he figured he wouldn't take any chances—"is your name Tom?"

"They calls me Tom," the old man said. "What of it?"

"Oh, nothin', nothin' atall . . . but, well, we heard stories—"

"What kinda stories?"

Walter took a deep breath. "Is it true you're lookin' for treasure?"

Tom snorted. "Ain't met the man yet who weren't."

"Yes, sir. But what I mean is—" Walter hesitated, then plunged on. "Was your father's name Lafitte?"

Tom's eyes became narrow slits. "Who wants to know?"

"Why, just us. I'm Walter Carroll, and this here's Alice."

Tom leaned forward confidingly. "Can y'all be trusted?"

"Well, yes, sir," said Walter.

"Both of you?" Tom looked at Alice.

"I'm *nine* years old," she said indignantly, as if that answered his question.

"Well . . ." The old man paused. Then he grinned. "Ask me no questions, I'll tell you no lies."

"Teacher says if you don't ask questions, you never learn anything," said Alice.

"That's so, that's so." Tom nodded. "But if you tells all you know, you ain't got no secrets left. Now me," he continued, "I got a whole sackful of secrets." He closed one eye and held out his gunnysack. "I got dreams to sell—fourteen-carat mysteries, better than gold. . . . Anything you ever want, right here in this old sack. Naw, now, no fair peekin'—you ain't paid yet. Nobody gonna get his heart's desire without he pay first. Come on, now, who got a nickel? Nickel buy you a smile, silver dime for twice as many, two bits have you laughin' right out loud. . . ."

Walter was taken aback. "We got no money, Mister."

The old man gave a low laugh. "Nobody ever do. Never mind, just habit. . . . Y'all fed me a fine meal; I s'pose I owes you least one secret."

Walter leaned forward breathlessly, forgetting to be afraid, while Tom groped about in the sack and muttered to himself. "Lessee, now, how's that? Naw, not that one . . . that don't do atall . . . maybe this?

Naw, we can do better . . . hmmm . . ." Finally he held out the sack to Alice. "Look like I need some help, Missy. What say you reach in and pull somethin' out—anything atall—and if it's a secret worth tellin', I'll tell it."

"All right," Alice began, and reached her hand out, but then she stopped. "You—you ain't got nothin' in there that *bites?*" she asked doubtfully.

Tom scratched his head. "Not last I looked. . . . But if you're scared—"

"I'm not scared!" Alice jutted out her chin and put her hand in all the way. When she drew it out again, she was holding an oddly shaped piece of wood.

"Why, it's just some old driftwood," she said. "That don't count, does it? Cain't I try again?"

"Up to you," said Tom, and he held the sack open for her to drop the thing back inside. "I guess if you don't care to hear 'bout it . . ."

"Wait—please," said Walter. "Does it have a story?"

"Ever'thing have a story, boy. Stories hangin' 'round all over the place, if you got eyes to see, ears to hear. Trouble is, most folks is blind and deaf."

"Tell us, please."

The old man looked at Alice. "Missy?"

Alice hesitated. Walter elbowed her. She gave him a disgusted look, then turned back to Tom. "Yes, please."

Tom grinned again. "Y'all look it over," he said. "See what kinda eyes you got."

Alice studied it one way, then leaned her head to the side and studied it another. She shrugged and handed it to Walter. "Just some old driftwood," she muttered.

Walter ran his fingers over the wood.

"How's it feel?" asked Tom.

"Smooth," said Walter. "Heavier than you'd think." He held it up before his eyes.

"What you see?" Tom asked.

"Looks like—oh, I don't know—a horseshoe, maybe, or a broke-off wishbone."

"Turn it over."

Walter did. On this side there was a big crack running through the wood, a long, skinny squiggle that started on one leg of the thing and curved up around the middle, ending up in a larger, hollowed-out place that was roughly heart-shaped. He looked at it long and hard.

"Is it—a face?" he asked finally.

The old man winked. "You got good eyes, boy." He lowered his voice. "Got a man's whole life trapped right inside this here wood. You can read it, same as readin' a hand, or tea leaves in a cup. Conjure woman show me how."

"Whose life?" asked Walter.

Tom just grinned. "Looka here," he said, "this where he's born, slap in the middle of a old herrycane—devil storm outa the Gulf—see there? Devil blow in with it, want to gobble him up, but his mama, she ain't afraid of nothin'. She say, 'Go on, y'ole devil—this child mine!' So the devil, he go 'way—but not for long. He mad; he bide his time. First chance he get, he carry off the mama instead."

"You mean she died?" Alice asked sympathetically.

Tom shrugged. "You tell me, Missy—look like that what the wood say. . . . Now the line go straight for a

little while—child grow up to be a man. But he a fool—
he say, 'Come on, devil, I fight you now.' But the devil,
he just laugh—see them old crossways gulleys? That's
the devil, laughin' his head off. Then he say, 'Come on,
fool, let's play us a game.' The devil, he like games,
but he all the time cheat. Fool say, 'What you mean?'
Devil say, 'I done hid a treasure, fool. If you find it, you
a free man. Rich, too. But if you cain't, you mine.' The
fool, he say, 'That ain't no kinda game. How I'm gonna
find that treasure?' He a fool, you see, but he ain't
ignorant. Devil say, 'Here your clue, fool—this treasure's
hid upside my bathtub.' So the fool, he go to the conjure
woman, ask what that mean. She say old Gulf's the
devil's bathtub, ever'body know that. Fool say, 'What
should I do?' Conjure woman, she pick up this here
piece of driftwood and conjure over it, then she point
right here, boy—in that face you seen—and shake her
head and tell the fool he might as well go on and play
the devil's game. She say, 'Look like it's the onliest
chance you got, fool. They's dead man's bones, showin'
through that face . . . that's the mark of the devil, sure
'nough. He gonna come crawlin' outa the Gulf again
someday, make another herrycane, carry ever'body off
this time—old fool, too. . . .'"

Tom recited the tale in a kind of melancholy sing-
song, as if he had said it all a hundred times before,
moaning a little and rocking his body from side to side.
But now he paused and leaned forward, looking from
one of them to the other. They sat frozen, staring at
him. Alice had a death grip on Walter's left elbow. . . .

Suddenly Tom began to laugh, and then the gulls

were laughing too; the air rang with the sound of laughter. The gold tooth gleamed. Tom laughed and laughed and laughed some more. . . .

Why, he's just nutty as a fruitcake, thought Walter, *nothin' but a crazy old coot, after all.* . . .

Tom stopped laughing. "You think I'm crazy, boy?"

Walter colored guiltily. *Good Lord, he can read minds!* "No—no, sir—"

"You lie," said Tom, but he sounded cheerful. "Missy here, she tell the truth. You think old Tom's crazy, Missy?"

Alice was worthless as a liar, it was true. "Well, not—not all that much . . ." she stammered. Walter nudged her. "I mean, hardly atall . . ."

The old man nodded. "Well, maybe I am," he said. "Maybe I am, but then again maybe I ain't, and if I ain't, they all gonna be laughin' out t'other side of they mouth one day, that's what. I got secrets, you see. . . ." He patted the sack and nodded knowingly. Walter held out the driftwood, thinking Tom wanted it back.

"Naw," he said, getting to his feet. He was surprisingly agile. "That's y'all's. I got to go now. . . ."

"Will you—come back again?" The words tumbled out before Walter could stop them; they surprised him more than anybody.

The old man's eyes gleamed for a moment with suspicion. Or was it amusement? Walter worried. "Depend on which way the wind blow," Tom answered. "Why you want me to come back?"

"Well . . . we could get you some more food—if you wanted it, that is—and maybe we could talk some more. . . ."

He made a kind of growling noise. "Tell the truth, boy—you after my treasure, that it?"

"No, sir." Walter's voice cracked. He cleared his throat. "I was only wonderin'—"

"Wonderin's next door to wantin'," said Tom. "Believe me, I know." He considered them for a moment longer. Then he tipped his battered hat. "I thank you for the fine breakfast." Next thing they knew, he was walking off slowly, down the beach. Crockett followed him a little way; then Tom leaned over and spoke to him, and the dog turned around and trotted back to Walter's side. He sat down in the sand, whimpering.

"Hell's bells," breathed Walter, when the tramp was just a shadow in the distance. "If that don't beat all . . ."

"Did you hear what he said, Walter?" Alice whispered, though there was no need to whisper. "Did you hear what he said about his treasure?"

"I heard."

"Lord, I like to died when he said that! Didn't you just like to die?"

Walter didn't answer. He jumped down into the hole that Tom had dug and kicked at the bottom with his foot.

"Anything there?" asked Alice.

Walter shook his head. There was nothing, just sand and a little water. He climbed out of the hole and squatted down by Crockett. "Not a thing," he said thoughtfully, gazing out at the Gulf. It was still and blue again today. Everything was the same. Nothing was the same.

"He sure had strange eyes, didn't he, Walter?" Alice shuddered. "Mighty strange eyes . . ."

"It was like he could look right into my head and read my mind," Walter murmured.

"Maybe he's been drinkin' moonwater!"

"Naw, that was just play-like, Sister. Old Tom's *real!*" There was a note of triumph in Walter's voice. "And you saw how it was with Crockett. Why, he never even barked at him, acted just like he was an old friend, didn't you, boy?" Walter stroked the dog's head. "I tell you, I never seen anything like it!"

"Well, I know—I saw him first, didn't I?" Alice picked up a shell and threw it into the hole. "Boy, I cain't wait for Sunday. Audie Merle Wise just won't believe it when I tell her—"

Walter looked up in alarm. "You cain't tell Audie Merle Wise or anybody else, you hear me? You cain't breathe a word about this!"

"Well, why not?"

" 'Cause people'd start talkin', and first thing you know somebody'd say somethin' about it to Mama, and you know how nervous she gets."

"I guess you're right. . . ." Alice's forehead puckered into worried lines. "Lord, Walter, what's Mama gonna say about all that food that's gone?"

"I'll just have to say I ate it, that's all. Well, you don't have to look like that—it's not the same as lyin'. I just won't eat as much myself at dinner. Anyhow, we're just feedin' the hungry, same's it says in the Bible."

"I guess so. . . ."

The two of them sat in silence for a while. Walter turned over the smooth wood in his hand and ran his finger along the squiggly line until he touched the thing that was like a face. *They's dead man's bones, showin' through that face . . . that's the mark of the devil, sure 'nough.*

"Lordy," he murmured, "he sure warn't anything like I thought he'd be. . . ."

• Chapter 7

Walter hid the piece of driftwood under his mattress. He was afraid it might give him nightmares, but that night he dreamed of William, running and laughing. "You cain't catch me, Walter!" the little boy cried. "See how fast I run!" And Walter let him get away, pretending to try his hardest, just the way he used to do. . . . He chased him into another day, another memory, when Papa had taken them all down to visit the lighthouse at Port Bolivar. . . . Now they were climbing the stairs to the top, a million trillion stairs, too steep for William's short legs. . . . "Take my hand," Walter told him, but he wouldn't listen. "I can do it all by myself," he insisted . . . and suddenly he wasn't climbing anymore; he was flying, and Walter was flying too. . . . And all the time William was laughing, calling over his shoulder, "You cain't catch me, Walter! You cain't catch me!" Then Sam Houston crowed, and Walter woke up smiling though he couldn't quite remember why. The dream had already slipped away.

All that day he worked hard at his chores, even harder

than he would have if Papa had been home. He wanted
to earn his father's praise, but it was more than that. He
was trying to chase away a vague sense of guilt that was
somehow connected with old Tom. . . . Walter had
the uncomfortable feeling that, no matter what Papa
had said about the tramp's being harmless, he wouldn't
have been altogether pleased if he'd known what had
gone on yesterday. After all, it was because of the stories
about Tom that he had asked Walter to stay home and
keep an eye on things. Yet at the same time, the thought
of yesterday filled Walter with pride—how many other
boys could say they had actually faced up to Tom the
Tramp? Never mind that he had been scared stiff, that
if it hadn't been for Alice, he would never have done it.
All that really mattered was that he, Walter Carroll, the
heretofore chicken-livered, had not only looked old
Tom in the eye but had said howdy-do and got away
with it—alive, which was the best part.

Mr. Carroll returned from Galveston that evening
with presents for everybody: dusting powder for Mama,
a wooden duck for Emily, and the finest surprise of all
for Walter and Alice together—a genuine stereoscope
with a box of slides that showed pictures of the Pyra-
mids and the Sphinx and Queen Victoria and London
Bridge, to boot. "Why, it's not fallin' down atall!"
exclaimed Alice.

They sat up late looking at all of them, asking their
father endless questions about wonders he had actually
seen in his days at sea. Those weren't anything to sneeze
at—Casablanca and Constantinople and Santo Domingo
and New York City. . . .

"How could you stand to give it up?" Walter asked

him. "How can you sit still in Bolivar when you've been all over the world?"

"Well, son, that's just it—I've *seen* the world. Oh, it's a fine place, I'll grant you that. But a man needs a home and a family. . . ." Papa's eyes rested for a moment on his wife's dark head, bent over a pile of holey socks and buttonless shirts.

Walter felt a hot flush spreading up from his collarbone to his scalp. It was for Mama that his father had given up the sea; they all knew that. Walter had heard Cousin Jack tease about it sometimes. "Oh, you wouldn'ta known your papa back then, Walter. He was quite the gentleman rover, yes, he was. Why, he broke hearts from Maine to Maracaibo—"

"Oh, Jack," Mary Agnes would interrupt, "such talk!"

But Cousin Jack would only wink and go on. "It's the truth, so help me! Richard Carroll was a well-known rapscallion, until the day he took one look at your mama's pretty eyes, and that was that . . ."

"How were all your relatives, Richard?" she asked now, her voice distant, almost formal. She had borne her husband's coming-home kiss with a rigid face. Walter had seen it, though he hadn't wanted to.

"Oh, fine, just fine," Papa answered, a little too heartily. "Jack and Mary Agnes are doing right well, and the twins are all still like as peas. . . . The youngest pair's just beginning to talk, and they tell me K. K. and Bussy are reading already—isn't that something? They're not even in school yet, you know—just the same age as—" He broke off abruptly, his face suddenly stricken.

"As William," his wife finished for him. "Yes, I remember."

There was a moment's painful silence, and then Papa said quietly, looking down at his fingernails, "I miss him too, Lillie. Don't you know I miss him too?"

"Looka here, Mama, you want to see the Leaning Tower of Pisa?" Alice asked anxiously.

"Some other time, Sister." Mama's voice was strained.

"But, Mama, it's real pretty—"

Their mother shook her head. "You children ought to have been in bed long ago. I don't know what I was thinking of. . . . You go on now."

"Yes, ma'am."

They pecked her cheek and went, but sleep was a long time in coming.

"Walter," said Alice, after a while, "you awake?"

Walter sighed. "Looks like it."

"Walter—"

"What?"

"Does Papa love Mama more'n she loves him?"

Walter got up on his elbow and glared at his sister. "You hush your mouth, Alice. You don't know what you're talkin' about!" he whispered fiercely.

"Well, it just seems like it sometimes. I was only askin'." Alice's voice trembled.

"Well, don't ask," Walter growled. "It ain't any of our business, anyhow. I swear, sometimes you got no more sense than a doodle bug."

There was a long, shuddering sigh from the next bed. Walter could see Alice's shoulders shaking, her head buried in her pillow.

"Aw, come on, Sister, don't do that. . . ." He hated it when she cried; seemed like it was always his fault somehow every time she did.

"I c-cain't help it—you're just so doggone m-mean!" She was sobbing now.

"Hell's bells . . ."

"Don't you c-cuss, Walter Carroll!"

"Aw, for cryin' out loud . . ." Walter climbed from his bed and sat down on the side of hers. "I'm sorry, Sister. Come on, please don't cry any more." He put his hand on her shoulder and patted it awkwardly. "I know what you mean about Mama and Papa. . . ."

Alice turned over and looked at him. "You d-do?" she hiccupped.

"Aw, heck, yes, but you just cain't worry about it, is all. Why, our folks is nothin' compared to some. You take Jimmy Jordan—everybody knows his mama hasn't spoke one word to his papa in five years. And you heard about Mr. Wesley Sparks, acourse—"

"Well, he died, didn't he? Ain't Miz Sparks a widder?"

"Shoot, no—she's nothin' but a grass-widder. They say she pestered Mr. Sparks so much that one day he just couldn't stand it any longer; he run off to California and grew a beard and became a Catholic."

"No!"

"It's the truth, I swear. So you see, Mama and Papa's all right. They're just goin' through a bad time, is all. . . ."

" 'Cause of William?"

"I guess." Walter didn't want to talk about that. It made his stomach hurt.

They were quiet for a minute. Then Alice spoke again. "Walter—"

"What?"

"Would you cry if I died?"

"Good Lord, Alice!"

"Well, would you?" She was feeling better now. Walter could tell.

"Nope," he answered. "Not a drop."

"Not a single drop?"

"Nope."

"Well, why not?"

" 'Cause I'd tickle you, like this, and then you'd come alive again—"

And then there commenced such a shrieking and giggling and tossing of pillows that Emily woke up and started to howl, and from somewhere under the house Crockett began to bark, and the next thing they knew Mama was shushing the baby and Papa was standing there fussing.

"What's going on in here? You ought to be ashamed of yourselves, both of you—carrying on so and waking the baby! Now, you all hush up right this minute and go on to sleep—you hear me?"

"Yes, sir."

"Yes, sir."

"Try to do something nice for you and this is how you behave. I ought to just smash that fool stereoscope with an axe, that's what I ought to do. . . . I better not hear one more sound out of this room, do you hear me?"

"Yes, sir."

"Yes, sir."

"Well, all right then. Good night."

" 'Night."

" 'Night."

Papa and Mama carried the baby off to their room, and everything was quiet again. There was only the sound of the wind on the sea, the waves breaking on the beach. . . . Walter's eyes closed. His whole being teetered on the brink of sleep. . . .

"Walter?"

Lord! "What?"

"You s'pose we'll ever see old Tom again?"

"I don't know, Sister." Funny, Walter had forgotten all about Tom for—what? Four, five hours? Suddenly he was wide awake again. "You better go on to sleep," he whispered. "Papa'll be comin' back in here, raisin' Cain."

"All right," said Alice. " 'Night, Walter."

" 'Night."

After a while Walter could hear her breath, slow and even, quivering only now and again with unspent sobs, and he knew she was asleep. But still he lay awake with wide-open eyes, watching the moonlight make shadows on the wall.

• Chapter 8

It was raining pitchforks.

"Well, that's funny, Miz Long—how'd you get in here?" Walter ducked breathlessly into the barn, milk pail in hand. "I thought you'd be waitin' outside." He was feeling fine. For three weeks the sun had scorched the earth with an unrelenting heat, while he and Papa struggled to clear a new field for fall planting. But it looked as if there would be little work this morning.

"Funny," he said again, drawing up the milking stool beside the cow, "I coulda sworn I closed that door last night."

"You closed it all right," said a voice from the shadows.

Walter very nearly fell off the stool. "Hey, Tom," he managed to croak, over the lurching of his heart.

"Hey, boy," said Tom. The gold tooth flashed. He was sitting Indian-style on the ground. Crockett lay contentedly beside him.

"I thought—I thought maybe you'd gone away," Walter stammered. It had been three whole weeks, after all; they were well into August now. The memory of Tom had already begun to fade and blur into unreality, to grow more comfortable, viewed from a safe distance.

Tom shrugged. "Wind shifted." There was certainly nothing safe or comfortable about him now. He was alarmingly real.

"Oh," said Walter.

"You better see to your cow," Tom said after a moment of silence.

"Oh—oh yeah. I guess I better."

Jane Long was as calm as Crockett about Tom's presence, paying him no more mind than she would have a fly—less, in fact; for a fly, she'd have switched her tail at least. But Walter was shaking so that the milk kept squirting in all directions, missing the pail nearly as often as not. His mind was racing. What should he do? What should he say? It was his own fault that old Tom was here; Walter knew that. He had invited the devil to dine, and, lo and behold, the devil had come! But what now? Lord have mercy—what now?

"Would you—like somethin' to eat?" Walter asked at last, when the pail was as full as he could get it.

"If it ain't no trouble—"

"Oh, no trouble—no trouble atall!" Walter lied. "Let me just—just take this milk on in to my folks. My mama's cookin' breakfast right now. Soon as it's ready, I'll bring you out some, how's that?"

"Well, long as you got plenty."

"Oh sure, we got plenty. One thing we got, it's plenty." *Hell's bells, I'm babblin' like a bubblehead,* Walter told himself as he backed out of the barn door.

Mama was frying eggs for breakfast. "Raining pretty hard out there?"

"Yes'm, pretty hard," said Walter, wishing his cheeks wouldn't burn so. Lord, but his mother would just keel over and die if she knew who was sitting in her barn. Walter's head felt heavy, as if his worries were rocks, weighing it down. "Where's Alice?" he asked, trying his best to sound casual.

"She's mindin' the baby," Mama answered. "Will you run get her for me, son—tell her we're about ready here?"

"Yes, ma'am."

Walter fairly burst onto the sleeping porch. "Alice, Mama sent me to tell you to come eat now, but listen to me—you cain't finish it all, you hear?"

"Well, why not, for heaven's sake? I'm hungry as a horse."

" 'Cause you got to save some in your napkin, same as me, that's why." Walter's voice squeaked like a rusty hinge. "Old Tom's come back!"

Alice's eyes bugged out. "You don't mean it!"

"Yes, I do too. He's sittin' right out there in our barn this very minute, and I promised we'd feed him again, so we got to."

"Lord, Walter, what if Mama finds out he's here? What if Papa goes out to the barn?"

"Mama's not gonna find out long as we don't tell her," he said, "and I don't think Papa'll have any reason to go out there with it rainin' like this. We just got to keep our heads, that's all."

"All right, Walter, I'll keep my head. I sure will!" Alice's eyes glittered with excitement.

"Well, come on then, startin' right now. You got to
act natural, you hear me?"

"I hear you—I hear you."

Alice was cool as silk during breakfast, but Walter
was so nervous that he spilled his milk twice and
knocked the butter dish on the floor and finally tipped
over the salt.

"Merciful heavens!" his mother cried. "Quick, son—
stand up and throw some over your left shoulder and
turn around twice!"

"Oh, Mama—"

"Just do it, Walter. No sense taking chances."

"Yes'm." Walter sighed. But when he stood up, he
forgot about the food in his lap, and it went tumbling
to the floor, and everybody saw.

"Why, Walter Carroll, what do you mean by hiding
your breakfast in your napkin? Are you sick?"

Walter was covered with confusion. "No, ma'am, I'm
not sick. I'm just—just not hungry, is all. . . ."

"He was prob'ly just savin' some for Crockett, weren't
you, Walter?" Alice said, turning to him with a smile.

Finally he stammered, "Yes, ma'am, that's it. I saw
him out in the barn when I was milkin' the cow, and
I—I remembered that I had forgot to feed him last
night." This was Walter's second lie of the morning.
Crockett had eaten a prodigious dinner the night before.
But Walter couldn't help that. He shot Alice a marvel-
ing look.

"Lord, son, why didn't you just say so in the first
place?" his father asked. "There's no need for you to
go without for old Crockett's sake. We've plenty for all
of us and him too."

"Well, certainly," said Mama, shaking her head and heaping Walter's plate with more eggs and grits. "The idea! Now, you eat this good breakfast, Walter. I'll fix a nice plate of scraps for Crockett. Goodness, carrying on so over that old dog."

"How'd you ever think so quick, Sister?" Walter whispered as they dodged raindrops out to the barn.

"*Somebody* had to," she said. "Lord, I thought you were gonna give the whole thing away—and you told *me* to act natural."

Tom was still sitting right where Walter had left him. He grinned his gold-toothed grin and tipped his hat to Alice as the children came in the door. "Mornin', Missy." He looked at Walter. "Thought maybe you'd changed your mind."

"I wouldn't do that." Walter handed him the plate of food. "It's a little messy," he apologized, "but it's good."

"Aw, it's fine, real fine. Your mama must be a mighty good cook."

"Well, I should say," Alice said proudly. "My papa says her biscuits are light as a feather, and one time she won first prize at the fair for her fig preserves."

"Is that so?" said Tom, his mouth full. "Don't surprise me one bit." Crockett sat up and begged as pretty as you please. "Just like a little old show dog!" Tom grinned, giving him a nibble. Once again, he took his time over the meal.

"Mmm-mmm, that was fit for a king," he said when he was finished. "Now"—he peered at the children with his sharp old eyes—"what you all want to talk 'bout today?"

Walter was tempted to ask again about Lafitte and his treasure, but he remembered how touchy Tom had seemed about that before. "Oh, I don't know," he began. "Any old thing . . ."

"You got your secrets with you?" Alice asked.

Tom reached behind his back and pulled out his gunnysack. "Never go anyplace 'thout 'em. Lessee, now, Missy chose last time; your turn today, boy." He held the sack out to Walter. Without giving himself a chance to think of all the horrible things he might discover, Walter thrust his hand in. . . . His fingers touched something that felt rough, then something mushy—he shied away from that—and then they closed on something small and cold. . . .

It was a tarnished silver chain, with a little heart-shaped locket attached.

"Ohhh," breathed Alice, as Walter held it up to the faint light coming through the cracked door, "it's beautiful!"

"That it is." Tom sighed faintly. "That it is."

Walter turned it over gently in his hand. It must have been an elegant little heart once. On one side there was set in the silver a tiny butterfly, just alighting on a wide-open silver blossom. On the other side a slender vase held five silver roses.

"Does it open?" asked Walter.

The old man inclined his head, and sure enough, Walter found a tiny catch. He pressed it, and the heart opened up. Inside was a miniature of a man's face, much faded and spotted, so that it was hard to tell anything about him except that his hair had been black.

Jean Lafitte had had black hair. Everybody knew that.

Walter shuddered.

"Somebody walkin' over your grave," said Tom. "Let your sister see, boy."

Walter handed the heart to Alice. She touched the butterfly wonderingly. "Beautiful," she murmured, "so beautiful . . ."

"Tell us the story, please," said Walter.

Old Tom leaned back against the barn wall and closed his eyes. For a time there was no sound but the rain on the roof—not even the sound of breathing, as far as Walter could tell. A terrible thought stole across his mind. *What if this old man dies right here, right now? He's awful old—older'n God, like Alice said. . . . Oh, Lord, don't let him die. What in Sam Hill would we do with him?*

But just then Tom stirred and began to speak quietly.

"Long time ago, way 'cross the ocean—not just this here old Gulf but the big ocean, the one they calls Atlantic—they's a girl not much older'n you, boy—fourteen, maybe fifteen year old. She so pretty it hurt your eyes to look on her, and she dress so fine—red color and yellow color and blue like a peacock feather, all scrambled up ever' which way in her clothes. And she pretty on the inside too—kindest heart you ever see and god-fearin'. Not just one-god-fearin', neither—she ain't so stingy; she fear the sun-god and moon-god and god of ever' river and tree, and she done right by all of 'em. But her people—they at war, you see, brother 'gainst brother—and one night when she sleepin', enemy come to her village, kill all the old and sickly, carry off the young and strong, in chains. And the girl, she holler and try to fight, but it ain't no use. They sells her to the white man, all the same, right along with t'others."

Tom paused and shook his head thoughtfully, then continued. "Next thing she know, she on a ship, big like a beast, with her in its belly. And she sick—they all sick, moanin' and cryin'—she cain't never remember how long. But she don't die—she too proud to die. And then one day different white men come on the ship—t'others calls 'em pirates—and they's hollerin' and fightin' till the first ones all dead. And these pirates, they takes the girl and all her brothers and sisters to a camp they calls Campeachy, what was on Galveston Island, and they sells 'em off, one by one. But the girl, she still so pretty that one of the pirates, he say, 'Don't sell her.' He want her. So she his woman now, and he kind to her, dress her in fancy clothes and give her this here silver heart, with his picture inside. And after a while, she be carryin' his child. Then the old herrycane come, blow down the pirate camp, kill off white and black, just alike—kill 'em like flies. But the girl, she live, and her child what's born that same night, he live too. . . ."

Tom paused again. Walter and Alice looked at each other with burning eyes.

"Now the pirates what's left alive looks around 'em and say, 'How we gonna feed us? Look like they ain't 'nough food and water to go 'round.' And the boss pirate, the one they calls Lafitte, he say, 'Too many niggers, that what's wrong. We got to sell off the ones

what's left.' So he take 'em all—girl and her child, too—
and he load 'em in the belly of another boat, send 'em
off to New Orleans. Next day they all sold, ever' last
one. White man from up the river, he buy the girl and
her child. He ain't much of a man, but his wife a
Christian woman—teach the girl 'bout cookin' and
cleanin' and mindin' white babies, teach her pretty
stories 'bout Jesus too. Take away the fancy dress the
pirate give her, make her wear clothes white lady call
decent. Woulda took away the silver heart, too, but the
girl, she smart, she hide it. And when her child get big,
she show it to him, tell him the story. She say they's
plenty more where that come from. His daddy done
buried it, but it's rightly his. He got to find it someday.
She say, 'You listen real good now 'cause I's sick, gonna
die, so you got to remember.' Child, he say, 'You cain't
die, Mama.' But she say, 'Look like I cain't help it.'
And then, sure 'nough, she die. . . ."

For a moment the word seemed to hang in the air.
Then it was swallowed by the sound of the rain. Alice
began to cry softly.

"Shh," Walter murmured, patting her back without
knowing he was doing it, "shh . . ."

Tom opened his eyes. "What you cryin' for, Missy?
All happened long time ago, ain't no never mind now."

Alice didn't answer. She couldn't stop crying.

Dimly, Walter realized that the silver heart was still
lying open in his hand. He closed it carefully and gave
it to Tom. "We cain't keep this," he said. "Wouldn't
be right."

"No"—Tom shook his head slowly—"wouldn't be
right. . . ." He sat looking at the necklace for a minute

or two. The chain was snarled. Carefully, almost tenderly, it seemed to Walter, the old man untangled it and put it in his shirt pocket. He stood up. "I best be goin'. Your papa gonna be comin' in here after a while, lookin' for y'all. He don't want to find Tom."

Alice looked up at him through her tears. "How do you know?"

There was a shadow of the old grin. "I know, that's all." Tom cocked his head. "Looka here, Missy, cain't leave you seemin' so sad, me with my belly full of your food. Lessee, now . . ." He peered into the gunnysack again, then pulled out a string of white shell beads and handed them to Alice, who wiped her nose on her sleeve.

"They're real pretty," she said, looking them over with drying eyes.

"Indians used to wear 'em," said Tom.

Walter's pulse, which had slowed to the lulling rhythm of the story of the silver heart, began to pick up speed again. "What Indians would that be?" he asked.

"Attacapa," said Tom. "It was the Attacapa that lived 'round here, mostly." A sly look crept back into the old eyes. "You all know what Attacapa mean?"

"No, sir."

"Eaters of men," said Tom, and now he really was grinning. "Choctaw call 'em that. Beach is full of they leavin's—arrowheads, broke-up pots, bones . . ."

Walter swallowed hard. "Bones?"

"Don't you like bones, boy?" Tom chuckled. "Whole history of the world writ in bones. All of us ends up bones sooner or later. . . . Y'all ever visit the Injun graveyard?"

The children shuddered and shook their heads. They knew that there was an old Indian graveyard some miles up the beach near Caplen. Everybody knew that, but no one in his right mind would consider visiting it. It was common knowledge that the graveyard was haunted by the spirits of two old chiefs who had died from eating the flesh of children, then taken on the form of snow-white owls. When Lester Barrett was a schoolboy, he used to claim that he had actually seen and spoken with them and just barely escaped with his life. There were those who tended to doubt this story, but nobody had ever felt inclined to put it to the test.

"Mighty int'resting place," Tom continued, "mighty int'resting. Them old Injuns buried there all dressed up, just like they goin' to a party. Buried with all they pots and pans, dried-up food, too, case they wakes up hungry, toys for the chirren, case they wants to play. But they don't never wake up; they all just dead as sticks, same's we gonna be someday. Sometimes I sleeps over there, so's I can get used to how it feel."

Alice's mouth dropped open in horror.

Walter laughed nervously. "Aw, he's just kiddin' us, Sister—ain't you, Tom?"

Tom winked. "Maybe . . ." He picked up his shovel and slung the gunnysack over his shoulder. "Y'all take it easy, now."

And he was gone.

• Chapter 9

The first chance they got, the children hid Alice's shell beads under Walter's mattress, with the piece of driftwood. Old Tom was on their minds most all the time now. In the dark of the night, while the rest of the family lay sleeping, they would speak of him in whispers.

"Seems like he's more than just one old man," Walter told Alice. "Soon's you get him figured out one way, he turns 'round and says somethin' that knocks your eyes out, gets you all confused again, till you don't know if you're comin' or goin'."

"You think he tells the truth?"

"Some of the time, maybe—maybe never—who knows? Maybe *he* don't even know."

"Sometimes he scares me," said Alice, shivering and drawing the covers up around her chin.

"I know," said Walter.

"But I like him."

"I know." Walter sighed helplessly. "Me too. Guess he's got us hypnotized, same's he does old Crockett."

"Walter?"

"What?"

"You think that girl in the story—the one that died—you think that was his mama?"

"I was sure thinkin' she was. Looks like that's what he wants us to think. . . . But then, I don't know, looks like he wants us to think he sleeps in graveyards, too."

"Well, maybe he does."

"Aw, Sister—"

"Well, *maybe* . . ."

"Well, he'll prob'ly be back 'fore long, and you can ask him yourself. 'Pears to me he's mighty fond of Mama's cookin'."

But a whole week plodded by, and there was no further sign of Tom.

By the following Saturday the new field was nearly cleared. Walter and Papa were trying to convince Dowling that he really did want to haul away one last load of trash, when Rupert Bland and Frank Buvens came by on horseback. They were carrying their shotguns. Walter felt, more than saw, his father stiffen. Papa didn't care much for guns.

"What say, Rupert, Frank?" he called out pleasantly enough. "Hot day for a ride."

"It's hot, all right," Mr. Bland agreed, "but we got some business to attend to that we thought you might be interested in."

"Well, why don't y'all come on in the house and cool off? Have a glass of lemonade—"

"No, thank you, Richard," said Mr. Bland. "Wouldn't want to put Miss Lillie to any trouble; we're just stopping for a minute. Wanted to warn you about that old black tramp. Looks like he's stealing chickens now."

"Old Tom?" Papa looked surprised. "Somebody see him?"

"Well, sure. You remember Lester said he saw him over't the old Peterson place a few weeks back. And several others have seen him since."

"Seen him stealing chickens?"

"Well, not exactly," Mr. Bland admitted, "but it comes to the same thing. Frank and me have both had chickens disappear lately, and to our way of thinkin' it's mighty suspicious-lookin' for that to happen just when that old darky's in the neighborhood."

Papa scratched his neck. "Well, I don't know, Rupert. Might have been an animal that got 'em—muskrat, maybe, or even a dog."

"Well, don't you see, that's just it," said Frank Buvens, putting in his two cents. "If it had been somethin' like that, our own dogs would have chased it off or at least barked and woke us up. But they never made a sound"—Here he leaned over his horse's neck and lowered his voice, as if afraid the wrong ears might hear what he had to say—"and everybody knows old Tom has some kind of power over animals that can keep 'em quiet if he wants it that way."

Walter thought of Crockett.

"So what are you all planning to do about it?" Papa asked.

"We're gonna catch him—that's what we're gonna do," said Mr. Bland. "Lester ought to be the one to do it; he's the deputy. But he's always off on that boat, so looks like it's up to us. We'll catch him and take him over to High Island. They can lock him up over there, or hang him, either one—we don't much care, long as we're rid of him."

Papa coughed. "I don't believe they hang men for chicken stealing, Rupert."

"More's the pity," said Mr. Bland. "Well, we got to be going. Just wanted to let you know how things stand. . . ."

"You all haven't seen old Tom on your property, have you?" Mr. Buvens asked.

"No, we haven't," Papa replied.

The men looked at Walter. He could feel the purple splotches beating their accustomed path up his neck. "No, sir," he said, hoping that no one would notice his peculiar color.

The men didn't pay him any mind. Mr. Bland was looking at his father again. "You, uh, you don't own a gun, do you, Richard?"

"Never had any use for one, Rupert," he answered calmly.

Walter felt half-proud, half-embarrassed. He knew he shouldn't care, but it galled him to see Mr. Bland sitting there looking so high and mighty.

"Well, if you should happen to see the tramp, don't let him out of your sight, and let us know soon as possible. You could send your boy, here."

"We'll keep our eyes peeled," Papa said.

"We'd appreciate it," said Mr. Bland. He turned his horse around.

Mr. Buvens tipped his hat and followed. "Give our regards to Miss Lillie and the little girls."

"Tell them not to worry about a thing," Mr. Bland

called over his shoulder. "I'm sure we'll have this whole situation taken care of in no time."

"I'll do that." Papa nodded.

He and Walter watched silently as the men rode away. "Rupert Bland always did want to be a Texas Ranger," he said, once they were out of earshot. "I guess old Tom's the closest thing to a criminal he can find on Bolivar Peninsula."

"Why does Mr. Bland hate him so, Papa?"

"Tom scares him, son. Any man's liable to hate what scares him."

"You think he really stole the chickens?"

"I wouldn't know about that one way or the other. But there's no sense in us worrying about it. Isn't any of our business, as far as I can tell. . . ."

BUT WALTER did worry. He couldn't stop worrying. Rupert Bland and Frank Buvens had been carrying guns. No telling what might happen if they found Tom. Even if they didn't shoot him, they'd take him over to High Island and have him locked up, and Walter had an idea that, for Tom, that would be every bit as bad, maybe even worse. . . .

"Goodness, Walter," Mama said at breakfast on Sunday, "you have circles under your eyes 'most down to your drawers! Didn't you sleep well last night?"

"Yes'm, pretty well," Walter said evenly. All night long the thought of the tramp had hovered on the edge of his brain like a mosquito that buzzes and buzzes and won't be swatted away. No matter how tightly he closed his eyes, he could see the old man grinning at him, hear Tom's crazy talk spilling around his ears like pieces of a

puzzle—*dreams to sell . . . you after my treasure? . . .*
she so pretty it hurt your eyes . . . eaters of men . . . that's
the mark of the devil . . . dead as sticks, same's we gonna
be . . . It had seemed to Walter that he'd just barely
drifted off when Sam Houston crowed and woke him
again.

His father looked up. "You sure you're all right, son?"
He lifted his chin. "You do look a little peaked. Have I
been working you too hard?"

"No, sir, I'm just fine."

Papa shook his head. "Boy your age oughtn't have to
work like a man. Couple more hauls as good as our last
and maybe we can afford to hire some help. How'd you
like that?"

"That'd be fine, Papa," Walter answered. Not that he
believed it for one minute. "But I don't mind the work."

"Course you got school starting in October; things
ought to be easing up around then, anyway."

"Yes, sir."

Mama was bustling about, filling a spoon with some
foul-looking concoction. "Here you are, son. Just take a
little of this and you'll feel made over. My father used to
have low blood now and again, you know, but he always
swore that a dose of sulfur and molasses would do the
trick every time."

"But, Mama, he *died*!"

"Don't be silly, Walter. It was old age killed your
grandfather, not this medicine. Now, open your
mouth—"

The sulfur and molasses tasted even worse than they
looked. "I don't know what everybody's fussin' about,"
Walter muttered. "I'm not a bit tired."

He fell asleep with his mouth hanging open during the church service. Dr. Croombs's sermons were guaranteed to have half the congregation nodding at the best of times; as it was, today Walter slept so soundly that he drooled. When Alice poked him in the ribs, it startled him so that he jerked awake and gave himself a crick in the neck. That was bad enough; what was worse still was that he felt dead certain both Lester Barrett and Fanny Kate Vaughan had seen. He turned red as a beet. It was beginning to feel like his natural complexion.

The church wasn't truly a church. The peninsula's permanent population was too sparse to warrant the building of a real one. Instead, the faithful gathered weekly in the dining room of the Patton Beach Hotel to doze through the doctor's words of wisdom, clench their teeth through Leola Sparks's hymn-singing, and check up on their neighbors afterward. With the distance between farms, Sundays were sometimes the only opportunity for socializing. At Mama's insistence, Walter and Alice and their father attended regularly, although Mama herself stayed home with the baby. She said it was because Emily was too young for church, but Walter suspected that the real reason was that she wouldn't have to listen to Mrs. Sparks sing. Walter himself felt reasonably certain that the pangs of hell would be easier to sit through than some of those high notes.

"And we should all of us, then, strive to be Good Samaritans likewise. . . ." Dr. Croombs droned on like an old bumblebee. Walter stole a glance at Fanny Kate Vaughan to keep himself awake. Lord, but she was pretty. She looked as if she had just stepped out of a bandbox, with her snow-white pinafore, her carefully

combed curls, her dainty little white-gloved hands folded
in her lap. Walter had tried a thousand times to imagine
how it would feel to be admired—or even noticed—by
such a creature; she was a year older than he was and
didn't know he existed. What would she say, he wondered, if she knew that he was on speaking terms with
Tom the Tramp, old Tom himself? Maybe she'd think
he was uncommonly brave, devilishly daring. . . . *Naw,
more'n likely she'd think I was uncommonly pinheaded.
Shoot, that's probably closer to the truth, anyhow.* . . .

"Puts me in mind of a story my mother once told
me. . . ." Dr. Croombs's voice was slow, soothing as a
lullabye. Again Walter felt his eyelids getting heavier
and heavier, the sharp edges of his consciousness beginning to blur. He stiffened the muscles in his neck and
gritted his teeth, but it was no use; a great wave of sleep
washed over him and he was drifting, drifting. . . . Now
Dr. Croombs was wearing Fanny Kate's pinafore. . . . No,
it wasn't Dr. Croombs, at all; it was Rupert Bland, that's
who it was—Rupert Bland, with Alice's Indian beads
around his neck and mayhaw jelly dribbling out of his
mouth . . . no, not jelly—that was blood, wasn't it? Somebody wipe it off, quick. . . . Not that Mr. Bland seemed
to mind much; he was just standing there, grinning, his
gold tooth gleaming. . . .

Gold tooth? Since when did Rupert Bland have a gold
tooth?

"Walter, wake *up*!" Alice whispered. "You're startin'
to snore!"

Walter opened his eyes just in time to see Lester Barrett looking straight at him with a smile that stretched
from one ear to the other.

"And now, Sister Sparks, if you would be so kind as to lead us as we lift our voices in song," Dr. Croombs was saying.

The hymn was "The Holy City." Lordy, Walter groaned inwardly. As if things weren't bad enough already, now he had to listen to Leola Sparks lay waste to Jerusalem.

> *Last night I lay a-sleeping,*
> *There came a dream so fair:*
> *I stood in old Jerusalem,*
> *Beside the temple there . . .*

Old Mrs. Sparks outdid herself today. There wasn't an eardrum for miles that was left unmolested. The congregation sat in stunned silence for a good half-minute after the final hosanna.

Well, at least church was over. Walter did his best to slip outside without drawing any more attention to himself, but Lester was waiting.

"Catchin' forty winks, huh, Romeo?" he teased him. "What's the matter—stay up too late dancing with your girl?"

Walter grinned the especially witless grin he saved for situations such as this. He'd have given his right arm for a clever reply; he knew from experience it would come to him hours later, too late to do him any good. As it was, he just stood there like a piece of cheese.

Lester clapped a hand on his shoulder and laughed. "Cain't say as I blame you; always been partial to yellow hair, myself." He lowered his voice. "Well, looka here, Romeo, it's the woman of your dreams comin' out the door this minute! Smile pretty, now. . . . Hello, Mr. Vaughan, Miz Vaughan. How are you this morning, Miss Fanny Kate? You know my friend Walter Carroll, don't you? Walter—well, where'd he get to?"

Walter had scooted behind an oleander bush, his heart beating furiously, his cheeks aflame. He didn't believe he could stand to face Fanny Kate Vaughan today. What if she laughed at him? Easier to just disappear for the time being. He peered out from between the branches and located his father, deep in conversation with J. N. LeBlanc. Well. It would be a while before he could escape altogether. The hotel yard rang with the usual Sunday morning pleasantries as neighbor greeted neighbor. Walter crossed his arms, leaned up against the white clapboard building, and waited. . . .

"Mornin', Miss Annie, Timothy. . . . Hot, isn't it? . . . You're lookin' well, Ashley. . . . Don't believe it's been this hot since . . . Hunter saw that long-tailed creature in our . . . especially fine sermon . . . Well, I was just saying to John Henry . . . you know that old darky's been after our chickens!"

Walter had been only half-listening, but now his ears perked up. He peeked through the oleander again. Rupert Bland was standing no more than two yards away, talking to Lester Barrett.

"I expect we'll be closing in on him any day now. There's Frank and myself and Ernest Atkins, and the Strathans have promised to help too. We'da had him before now, if dogs had done us any good. . . . Funniest thing about that old man and dogs—you ever hear that? It's like he's got 'em bewitched or some such."

"I tell you what," said Lester, "we'll just take my Samson, then. The man hasn't been born that could bewitch him."

Walter gulped. Lord, not Samson! Tom wouldn't stand a chance against that monster.

"Well, whatever you think, Lester—you're the deputy, of course. What do you say to a little hunt later on this evening?"

"Can't do it today, Rupert—already promised Bubba I'd take him to Galveston. What say Samson and I join you all tomorrow evening, if you haven't had any luck by then?"

"Well, that'd be fine, Lester. 'Preciate your help."

"Not atall. If there's one thing I can't tolerate, it's a thief. Speakin' of thieves, Rupert, did I ever tell you the story 'bout Lovan Hamshire's oldest girl runnin' off with the Thompson Seed salesman? No? Well, it seems there was this special on rutabaga. . . ."

Walter didn't pay any more attention after that. He wasn't in the mood for one of Lester's tales. First chance he got, he slipped out from behind the oleander.

"Well, there you are, son!" his father called out. "Come along, now. Your mother will be expecting us."

"Yes, sir," said Walter. The crowd had thinned out some; Fanny Kate Vaughan was nowhere in sight. But it wasn't Fanny Kate Vaughan Walter was worrying about now.

IT WASN'T FAIR, that was all. Rupert Bland, famous for nothing, and Frank Buvens and Ernest Atkins and now Lester Barrett and Samson, to boot—all of them against one old man. No way you could call that fair; it stank to high heaven, that's what it did. Walter was near to gagging with the smell of it.

But what business was it of his, anyway? Why did it matter to him what happened to some crazy old coot who was always mumbling a lot of nonsense about secrets and bones and digging for treasure that was likely no more'n a pipe dream? Walter asked himself that question over and over again as he sat on the beach that evening after supper, watching the waves break on the sand. Alice had tried to follow him, but he had run her off. He couldn't explain what he was feeling, couldn't put it into words to himself, much less to her. It was a kind of pain, almost—the same hard lump that stuck in his craw like a piece of undigested potato whenever he saw a half-dead animal caught in a trap or looked at that old black ribbon around his mother's neck. It wasn't fair, that was all.

Walter picked up a shell and drew a circle in the sand. The tide was out now. The sky glowed red, reflecting the sun that was setting behind his back. *Red sky at night, sailors delight.* . . . He added eyes and nose to the circle, then a grinning mouth. It wasn't very good, not much better than the faces William used to draw in the sand. He was always drawing faces. . . .

Walter sighed unhappily. He had thought the bad feeling would wash away here on the beach; other times, for other reasons, it had. But not today; it wasn't going anywhere today.

He added a tooth to the mouth and paused for a moment, considering its effect. Then, with one swift sweep of his arm he erased the whole thing.

I got to warn him, he told himself. *Some way or other, I got to warn him.*

• Chapter 10

Walter awoke with a start. He hadn't meant to fall asleep at all; what time was it, anyhow? He looked out the window. There was a little old sliced-off half of a moon just rising. *Moon like that won't rise till after midnight,* Walter told himself. *Looks like I've lost half the night. . . .*

He jumped out of bed without giving himself a chance to think about what he was doing, pulled on his britches, and started across the room. The floor creaked beneath his feet, and he froze. . . . Nothing. He moved again. He was past the girls' beds . . . past the bureau . . . almost to the door. . . .

"Where you goin', Walter?"

Hell's bells.

"Go on back to sleep, Sister. It's the middle of the night."

"Well, I know that. Where you goin'?"

"It ain't any of your business."

"Can I come with you?"

"No."

"Why not?"

" 'Cause it might be dangerous for a girl, that's why not. Now, you just go on back to sleep, you hear me?"

"Walter Carroll, if you don't tell me where you're goin', I'm gonna go wake up Mama and Papa."

"You wouldn't do that—"

"You just try me. I double-dog dare you!"

"For Gordon's seed," Walter murmured. He didn't have time to argue. "Look, I'm goin' to find old Tom and warn him they're comin' after him with dogs and guns, all right? Now, leave me alone."

Alice's eyes widened. "Who's comin' after him with dogs and guns?"

"Mr. Bland and Mr. Buvens and Lester Barrett and the Strathans—all of 'em. And they're settin' old Samson on his trail tomorrow. Don't seem fair to me, that's all. Look, I told you the truth, so just go on back to sleep."

Alice shook her head. "I'm goin' with you."

"You are not, either. I told you, it might be dangerous for a girl."

"I don't care. If you're goin', I'm goin'."

"Aw, for cryin' out loud." He had to take her. That was all there was to it. "Well, come on, then. I cain't stand here talkin' all night."

The truth was, he was glad of her company. The night was dark, thick with darkness. Clouds scudded across the sky like evil things, clawing at the moon. There was no light to speak of but the distant flashing of the old beacon down at Port Bolivar and the pallid glimmer of a star or two. The children ran alongside the Gulf, their ears full of its noise.

"Sure is dark," Alice panted, when they had gone a little way down the beach. "How're we ever gonna see him, anyway?"

"We got to look for a campfire, same as we saw that first night, 'member? That's the only way I can figure."

"Lord, Walter, he might be anywhere."

"I know, I know. But we got to try—"

Just then there was a greeting bark, and Crockett came bounding up behind them.

"Well, look who's here!" cried Walter. "Hey, boy, you want to help us find old Tom?"

Crockett wagged his tail.

"Aw, come on, Crockett—you remember Tom. Go find Tom!"

The dog cocked his ears questioningly.

"I don't think he knows what you're sayin', Walter."

Walter sighed. "I guess not. Well, come on, let's keep goin'."

They trotted on in silence. There was no campfire to be seen, nothing but that old lighthouse light blinking steadily up ahead, just as it had done every night for as long as Walter could remember . . . on again, off again, on again, off again. . . . He found himself trying to run, even to breathe, in its rhythm. And then, in his mind he was climbing again to the top of those winding stairs. . . . You could look out of the tower, once you got to it, through a spyglass they kept there for visitors. Seemed as if you could see the whole world from up so high. "Is that China over there?" Alice had asked on that long-gone holiday, and Papa had laughed and said no, probably just High Island. And he had pointed out their house, and the Sea View Hotel, and Barrett's Landing, and the old Indian graveyard. . . .

Walter stopped dead in his tracks. "Hell's bells," he murmured.

"What? What is it?"

"I bet I know where he is."

"Where?"

Walter felt sick. Weak at the knees. "In the Indian graveyard," he whispered.

Alice gasped. "No!"

"It just now came to me. I don't know why I didn't think of it before. He told us himself, 'member? He said he sleeps over there sometimes."

"But you said he was just makin' it up."

"Well, I know, but what if I was wrong? All of a sudden I got this terrible feelin' I was wrong. Maybe old Tom got to thinkin' how that might be a good place to find treasure. You never know—pirates coulda buried it right there with all them Indian bones and such. Wouldn't anybody want to go messin' 'round in a graveyard, see, so it'd be safe." Walter squatted down and began to pet Crockett, to steady himself. "Oh, Lordy, I just bet that's where he is!"

"But, Walter, ain't it haunted?"

Walter swallowed hard. "Aw, Sister, you don't really believe in them old ghost owls."

"N-no. . . . Do you?"

"Course not." For a moment neither of them spoke. Still as statues, they listened to the sound of their blood throbbing in their temples, their throats, even their fingertips. . . .

"I guess I got to go over there," Walter said at last.

"All right, then," said Alice. "We better get goin'."

"Not you, Sister, you don't have to go. I cain't let you go—"

Alice squared her shoulders. "If you're goin', I'm goin'."

Walter felt a kind of admiring exasperation. Was she really as brave as all that, or was it just that, next to him, a pussycat would have looked like a lion?

As if in answer, Alice put her hand in his. "It's all right, Walter," she said. "You'll take care of me."

It wasn't much of a graveyard—just a low mound, about fifty feet across, maybe three feet high in the middle, covered over with marsh grass and tall weeds and sticker bushes. It was thick with blackberries in June, but the birds had their pick of the crop; any Bolivar child would just as soon eat snake eggs as one of those Indian ghost berries.

"Shouldn't be too much fu'ther now," Walter panted, as they drew nearer the spot. It had taken them the best part of an hour of running to get this far. Once they left the beach, they had to cut across the marsh and on through Mr. Langdon Huett's property for the rest of the way. It seemed to Walter that his feet had grown heavier with every step. The wind had risen. It rustled through the marsh grass, sighing like a widow woman at a funeral wake.

"You know, I don't really see any sense in us goin'

right up onto the mound," Walter said, trying his best to sound matter-of-fact.

"Me neither," said Alice, her face white in the faltering moonshine.

"Good. Once we're close enough, we can just holler what we know. If Tom's there, he'll hear us."

"Well, sure," said Alice. "That's the way to do it, all right. . . ."

They were walking now. The ground was too rough for running.

"Walter?"

"What?"

"You didn't hear a kind of hootin' noise a minute ago, did you?"

"Naw . . . prob'ly just doves, that's all. . . ."

"Prob'ly so. . . ."

A minute passed. Two minutes.

Suddenly Crockett broke away, barking wildly.

"What's wrong with him?" Alice cried.

"Don't move," Walter whispered. He could just make out a huge, dark form moving slowly not ten yards away. The children stood frozen, their blood no better than ice water in their veins.

"Mooo," said the thing.

Walter nearly fainted with relief. "Aw, it's just one of Mr. Huett's cows." He rubbed his arm. "Lord, Sister, you like to've cut off my circulation!"

"Well, weren't you scared?"

"Naw . . . well, not all that much. Come on over here, Crockett. Leave that old cow alone!"

They circled cautiously around the cow and kept

going. The little snippet of a moon was higher in the sky now. It didn't part with much light, but it was better than nothing.

"You don't smell rain, do you?" Walter asked after a while, mainly for the comfort of hearing his own voice.

"I don't think so," said Alice.

"Well, that's good." They walked on in silence, slapping at mosquitoes. It was lucky there was a breeze, or the pesky critters would have been even worse. Walter began to wonder if he and Alice had got turned around somehow; surely they ought to be there by now. . . .

A cloud blew across the moon.

"Lord," said Walter. "I cain't see my hand in front of my face."

"Me neither."

"Just hold still for a minute, Sister; we don't want to trip."

"I cain't hold still—skeeters are eatin' me alive!"

"Well, wiggle around some and slap 'em. Moon'll be out again in a second, and then we can go on."

"You think we're almost there?"

"Bound to be."

Alice sniffled.

"Aw, come on, Sister. You cain't go to pieces now!"

"But I cain't see you, Walter—"

"I'm right here. Look, give me your hand again. . . . That's right."

"Where's Crockett?"

"He was here just a second ago. Crockett! Here, boy! Come 'ere, Crockett!"

There was no sound but the trilling of a thousand tiny insect voices and the low rush of the wind.

"Well, where'd he get to?" Walter grumbled. "Lord, I hope we find old Tom pretty soon. I cain't take much more of this. I wonder if—"

Just then the moon shook loose from the cloud, and the words died unspoken on Walter's lips. In the pale light he could see the figure of a man standing no more than spittin' distance from him and Alice. Crockett was sitting at his feet.

"Y'all lookin' for me?"

• Chapter 11

Old Tom had looked plenty fearsome before, in the daylight. Now, with only that flimsy excuse for a moon shining down on him, he was enough to scare the pants off a hero.

"What'sa matter, boy—cat got your tongue?"

Walter was shaking so badly he could hardly speak. "W-we came to w-warn you," he stammered. Alice was nigh to crushing every bone in his left hand.

"Warn me 'bout what?" The old man rubbed Crockett behind the ears. The dog gave a little groan of contentment.

Walter took a deep breath. "They're comin' after you —Mr. Bland and all of 'em—comin' after you with dogs and guns—say they're gonna lock you up. You got to get off the peninsula right now, right this minute—"

Tom eyed the boy warily. "What you talkin' 'bout, boy? What they wants with me?"

"They think you been stealin' their chickens."

Tom grunted. "Hmmph. That all?"

"Well . . ." Walter hesitated. "My papa says you—you sorta scare 'em, some way."

The gold tooth flashed. "But I don't scare *you*, that it?"

"N-no, sir."

Tom leaned forward menacingly. "Well, you b'long to be scared, boy," he growled. "What you thinkin' 'bout, draggin' your little sister out here in the dead of night? No tellin' what mighta happened!"

It was the last thing Walter had expected to hear. He had taken it for granted that Tom would appreciate having his life saved. "Well, I just—just thought you ought to know," he mumbled defensively. "They got *guns*, Tom . . . and they're gonna set old Samson after you tomorrow. He ain't like these other dogs, you know."

"Don't make no never mind, boy—they ain't gonna get Tom with dogs and bullets. Ain't nothin' gonna get him but the old Gulf hisself. Conjure woman don't lie."

"Just thought you ought to know, is all. . . ."

Tom narrowed his eyes. "Well, you thought wrong, boy. Ain't nobody askin' you for nothin'. What you think—I's gonna leave you my treasure when I pass? Hmmph. Look like you'da had more sense. Go on, now —take this child home! If I's your papa, I'd wear you out."

Shame and disappointment rose in Walter's throat. Why in blazes had he ever tried to help the old fool anyway? *Must have been out of my mind. . . .* He turned to Alice. "Come on, Sister. Let's get away from here."

Suddenly Alice jerked free of Walter and faced Tom.

"You got no call to talk to Walter that way, Mister. He's just tryin' to help you out. You got no call!"

Lord, thought Walter, *she's gonna get us both killed.* He reached for her arm. "I said come on, Sister—let's just go home—"

But for the moment Alice was too mad to be scared. She shook him off. "And he didn't drag me out here, neither. I made him bring me. And nobody's tryin' to steal your old treasure. I don't believe you're ever gonna find it anyhow!"

"*Alice!*" Walter hissed. "Come on, will you?"

Tom crossed his arms. It was too dark to tell for sure, but Walter suddenly had the impression he was grinning. "So you think I's too hard on your brother, Missy?"

"I sure do."

"And my treasure ain't nothin' but crazy talk—that right?"

Alice stood her ground. "That's right."

Tom chuckled. "Well, maybe so, maybe so . . . you mighty sure of yourself."

There was a sudden whirring, rushing sound, and something swooped out of the darkness close beside them. Alice shrieked.

"Get down! Get down!" Walter yelled, hitting the dirt and pulling her down with him. "It's the ghost owls— they're after us!"

To his amazement the night was suddenly filled with laughter—deep, rich laughter—Tom's laughter. "Ghost owls? What you mean, ghost owls? Looka there, boy, Missy—they owls, all right, but they ain't no more ghosts than you and me."

Slowly, tremblingly, the children got back on their feet and looked up where Tom was pointing. In the faint moonglow they could just dimly see a pair of huge white owls, circling serenely about twenty feet over their heads.

"We the ones trespassin', not them." Tom's voice was hushed now, almost reverent. "This they home."

For a moment nothing moved but the wind in the grass and those two great white birds up above.

"They're not—not the spirits of old Indian chiefs who died 'cause they ate babies?" Alice faltered at last, her voice small.

"Hmmph," Tom snorted. "Who tellin' y'all that kinda trash? Onliest Indians 'round here ain't botherin' nobody—they just dead, that's all. Lyin' there mindin' they own business right under your toes."

Alice gave a stifled scream and stumbled over her feet, trying to back up.

"What do you mean?" Walter cried. "This ain't the graveyard; we never got that far!"

"You wrong again, boy," said Tom. There was no question that he was grinning now. "We standin' slap in the middle of it."

THE CHILDREN turned and ran. They ran as if all hell gaped behind them, ran blindly, tripping and scrambling, mindless of the sticker-burrs that stabbed their feet, expecting every second to hear the rush of owls' wings about their ears, to feel the clutch of icy claws at their necks. Crockett ran with them, bounding along joyfully, barking at cows and nutrea rats alike.

The air was damp, clammy as a grave. It smelled of

dead fish. Sweat clung to the children's skin like old wet rags. Walter had Alice by the arm, dragging her along when she started to lag behind.

"Come on, Sister, you can do it—not much fu'ther now. Look there—you can see the beach over yonder. We're almost to the beach—"

Alice yelped and fell. One foot had slipped on a shell and turned under. She sat on the ground, holding her ankle, sobbing as much from fright and exhaustion as from pain. Walter knelt beside her.

"For cryin' out loud! It's not all that bad, is it? Aw, come on, Sister, cain't you get up? Here, lean on me—that's right. . . ."

"Ow—it h-hurts. . . ."

"Well, I know. Look, we can walk now—no need to run. Come on, Alice, we just got to get home!"

"I'm comin' fast as I c-can."

They limped along more slowly now, too worn out to speak. They had reached the beach. The tide was nearly all the way out. The moon had disappeared altogether behind the clouds that were blowing in off the water, but the sky was a little lighter, glowing dimly at the horizon. Every now and again it spat raindrops at them.

Suddenly Walter stood stock still. "Lord help us," he breathed.

"What is it? What's the matter?"

Wordlessly, he pointed. The beach made a gentle curve here, so that now the Carroll house was clearly visible about a half mile away, just beyond the sand hills.

From every window, yellow light streamed.

. . .

LILLIE CARROLL's heart was pounding in her ears. She couldn't stop the pounding, though she had willed it to stop—*ordered* it to stop at once. . . .

"What in the world were you thinking of, Walter?" Her husband's voice was taut with anger. Their son stood in the middle of the kitchen floor, hanging his head, while Richard stormed around him, hollering. "You just answer me that—what in the world did you think you were doing? Don't you know you both could have been killed? Didn't you even think twice about putting your little sister in that kind of danger?"

"Don't let him yell at Walter, Mama," Alice sobbed. "It was my fault, too. . . ."

But Lillie couldn't speak, couldn't say a word. She could only stand there, dumb with horror, holding the distraught child in her arms. . . .

"Scarin' your mother to death. She's worried herself sick—do you see that? And Alice's foot swoll up so bad— I tell you, I'm so mad, I can't see straight!"

Alice had spilled out the whole story through her tears; it was that which had left Lillie mute and shaken, set her heart pounding. It was like some awful nightmare —that horrible old man, talking to her children, breathing the very air they breathed, filling their heads with no telling what sort of vile things. Why, he was crazy— everybody knew that. A murderer, too, most likely. Lillie's head was reeling. She felt sick to her stomach.

Her husband was still shouting. "I told you, didn't I? I told you that old tramp was none of our business! Well, answer me, boy—didn't I tell you?"

"Yes, sir, you told me."

"Well then, why didn't you listen?"

" 'Cause Lester was gonna set old Samson after him. I heard him say so . . . and you said yourself that Tom never did anybody any harm—"

"Don't tell me what I know!" Richard exploded. "If you were so anxious to do the right thing, then why didn't you come talk to me about it? Why'd you have to go sneakin' around in the dark? I thought you had more sense than that, Walter—I sure did."

"I'm sorry, Papa."

"Well, sorry's not enough, you hear me? Sorry's nowhere near enough. You got to learn better, son. Go get me my belt. Go on—"

Lillie didn't stay for the belting. She knew it was necessary, had sometimes even thought that Richard was too soft with the children. "Spare the rod and spoil the child"—everybody knew that. But she couldn't bear to watch, all the same. Silently, she carried Alice away and tended to her foot, then bathed her scratches and mosquito bites and put her to bed on the porch beside little Emily, who had slept, for a wonder, through the whole episode.

"He ought to belt me too," Alice kept wailing. "It was my fault, too. . . ."

"Hush, Sister." It was all Lillie could do to form the words. "You just hush, do you hear me?"

The pounding had gradually diminished, given way to a growing heaviness, a dull throbbing behind the eyes that always signaled the beginning of one of her bad headaches. They had plagued her, off and on, all during the past year.

She passed Walter in the hallway. He went by her

without a word, his eyes averted. He wasn't crying, hadn't shed a tear, from the stiff-necked look of him. As Lillie stood staring, she felt a strange kind of distance, as if she no longer knew her own child. *God help me,* she asked silently, *have I lost another?*

Now her husband was beside her, putting his arms gently about her. "Come to bed, sweetheart. It's been an awful night, but it's over now. You ought to try and get some rest. . . ." His voice sounded hollow, drained. She knew he was sick at heart, now that his anger was spent. He loved his son deeply—any fool could see that. She ought to feel sorry for him, offer him some comfort. But she had none to offer. She felt nothing for him. She felt nothing but her own pain.

• Chapter 12

Walter woke to the sound of Sam Houston's crowing. "Dang rooster," he mumbled, dragging himself out of bed. "Seems like he'd get sick of hearin' himself . . ."

Fog was rolling in off the water. A pale gold sunrise struggled through it, thin and watery as chicken broth. "Prob'ly be hot as blazes again once this burns off," he told Jane Long, as he sat squirting the milk into the pail. "What you think 'bout that, Miz Long?"

Jane Long didn't seem to care one way or the other. She gazed off dreamily into space, chewing her cud.

He felt so empty—as if there would never be anything else to get excited about, to care about. His life stretched before him, dreary as one of Dr. Croombs's sermons. Funny, he hadn't realized how taken up he'd been with old Tom and his crazy talk, how they'd come to fill his heart and head with a kind of magic, a mystery that was gone now. . . .

"Mornin', son." It was Papa, walking out through the dewy grass, wanting to make up—to be friends again as if last night had never happened. That was his way.

"Mornin'." Walter didn't raise his head. He could feel his cheeks heating up again with shame, the smart of the belt still tingling on his legs.

"You feelin' all right this morning?"

"Yes, sir."

"Had a good long rest, didn't you?"

Walter looked up now, confused. Was his father teasing him? "Only 'bout an hour, wasn't it?"

Papa chuckled. "More like twenty-four, I'd say. It's Tuesday, son. You missed Monday altogether—didn't you know?"

Walter was amazed. He suddenly felt more rested. "No, sir. . . . I'm sorry—you had to do my chores, then."

"No matter." His father shrugged. "There wasn't that much to do. Rained off and on all day, anyhow." He looked as if there were something else he wanted to say, but then he appeared to change his mind. "You, uh—you 'bout done there?"

"Yes, sir."

"Well, that's fine. Mama's fixin' you a good breakfast. I'll, uh, I'll see you back at the house." He stood there for a moment more, fiddling with a button on his shirt-sleeve. Then he started to walk away.

"Papa—"

His father turned around. "Yes, son?"

"Did you hear if—if they caught old Tom?"

Papa shifted uncomfortably. "They caught him, all right. Lester'll be takin' him over to High Island sometime today. They kept him locked up in the boat shed overnight." He laid a hand on Walter's shoulder. "I'm sorry, son. I know you meant to help him. But I believe it's the best thing, after all. I don't know—maybe he really was gettin' crazy enough to be dangerous. Can't take a chance on something like that. . . ." He paused for a moment, cleared his throat, and went on. "Walter . . . I was with 'em. I was the one showed 'em where to look for him, in the graveyard. Your mother and I agreed I had to, after the scare we had. You see that, don't you?"

Walter stared blankly at his father. Surely he hadn't heard right.

"Don't you see I had to, son?" His voice was gentle.

"Yes, sir," Walter murmured. He did see—of course, he saw. Hadn't he been telling himself he didn't care what happened to the old man, that it wasn't any of his business, just like Papa had said in the first place? Well, sure . . . He was even glad that Tom had got himself caught—that's right—*glad*. Walter had tried to warn him. It wasn't his fault he wouldn't listen. . . .

Funny, though, thought Walter—*if it hadn't been for me trying to save him, maybe they wouldn't have found him, after all. Maybe old Samson would have turned out just like Crockett and all the others. Maybe Tom'd still be free as a bird, right this minute—free as those big old owls flying over the graveyard last night.* . . . *No, not* last night! *Lordy!* It was all so muddled. . . .

Some hero he had turned out to be. Some big hero. It was funny, that was all. *Funniest thing—*

So how come he felt so awful?

Papa cleared his throat again. "Well, I'll go on back now, tell Mama you're on your way in. I'll bet you're right hungry." ·

"Yes, sir," said Walter. But he wasn't hungry at all.

· · ·

NO ONE in the Carroll household spoke of Tom after that morning. It was as if they had all agreed silently that he was best forgotten now. But, try as he might, Walter couldn't forget him, couldn't throw off the sick feeling that came over him whenever he thought of the old man and his dad-blasted sackful of secrets. *It ain't my fault,* he told himself over and over again. *It ain't my fault they locked him up; I just tried to warn him, that's all. It ain't my fault he wouldn't listen. . . .* But he could still see Tom squinting at him and muttering, "You thought wrong, boy . . . ain't nobody askin' you for nothin'. . . . You thought wrong, boy, wrong, wrong, wrong. . . ."

Walter tried to ease his conscience by throwing himself into his work. All week he milked and weeded and hoed and turned melons like a man possessed, till even his hardworking father noticed and tried to slow him down. "Why, son, I believe these are the same melons you turned yesterday! No need to fool with them again so soon. You've been working too hard. Why don't you take this afternoon off, enjoy yourself a little? Water looks mighty inviting. . . ."

The water did look good. The weather had been perfect lately—full of blue skies and sparkling waves, sea grass bending in the Gulf breeze. But Walter's insides had ached too much for him to notice.

"Maybe you could take Alice for a swim," Papa went on. "Her ankle's looking better. Water might do it some good."

Walter flushed. "Don't really feel much like swimmin' today." He had avoided Alice as much as possible ever since the night of the graveyard. She couldn't really tag

after him much with her foot hurt, and that was all to
the good, as far as Walter was concerned; looking at her
only made him feel guiltier than ever.

Papa gave him a keen look. "Well, suit yourself, son.
But no more work today—that's an order, you hear me?"

"Yes, sir."

He settled on going wade-fishing. He thought for sure
that would take his mind off his troubles; it most always
did. But the fish had other plans that afternoon. He
never got a nibble, save for a couple of bony little catfish
not worth the time of day. And then, when he wasn't
paying good attention, a bloated purple monster of a
Portuguese man-o'-war floated by and stung the sweet
Jerusalem out of his left arm. Walter was feeling so low-
down by that time that he would have almost welcomed
the pain, if it just hadn't hurt so much. . . .

He was too big to go crying to Mama about it, but
Lord, how he wanted to—how he wanted to run to her
and bury his head in her lap, as he used to do when he
was little, and just cry and cry till he was all cried out.
But he was thirteen years old, for heaven's sake—practically a grown man. And anyway, Mama was shut up in
her room; she had been suffering all week with a sick
headache. So Walter shuffled through the medicine chest
himself and found the Tischner's Antiseptic and did the
best he could for his hurt without disturbing her.

That night he couldn't sleep a wink for the pain. His
arm was burning like fire, throbbing like thunder; the
rest of him was alternately hot and cold and altogether
miserable.

"Serves me right, serves me right," he moaned as he

tossed back and forth on his pillow, shivering beneath his covers one minute, throwing them off the next.

Alice heard him. "What serves you right? What's the matter, Walter?"

"It's my arm—it's killin' me . . . my own fault . . . I was wrong—he didn't ask me for nothin'. . . . Hell's bells, but it hurts, though. . . ."

Alice hobbled over to his bed in alarm. "You're sick, Walter. You're burnin' up with fever. I'm gonna get Mama."

Walter pushed up on his elbow and glared at her. "No, you're not. Don't you bother her, you hear me?"

"But Walter, you're sick!"

Now he sat up straight. "I'll tell you what's wrong with me—it's not my arm atall. It's that old man, Sister. He's drivin' me crazy—he's poisonin' me. . . ." Walter jumped out of bed and started groping under his mattress.

"Poisonin' you—what are you talkin' about?" Alice's voice was tight with fear. "What are you doin'? You ought to get back in bed."

But Walter had found Tom's driftwood and the Indian beads and was already carrying them across the room toward the door.

"Walter, come on back to bed. You don't even have your britches on!"

He didn't listen. He had to go down to the beach. He just had to. . . .

He felt a little better once he was outside in the night air. He ran like the wind, like a jackrabbit with the hounds after him, past Mama's garden, through the

marsh, across the sand hills, onto the beach. Crockett
was at his heels; he had heard him and come running
too.

The tide was just past full. From somewhere in the
darkness a lone seabird cried, disturbed out of its night's
rest.

"Walter! Walter, you all right?" Alice had followed
him, hopping along as best she could.

"Looka there, Sister—it's another moonwater trail,
ain't it—another blasted moonwater trail," Walter muttered, staring out at the water.

"What are you talkin' about, Walter? There ain't no
moon tonight—nothin' but stars—cain't you see?"

Walter blinked. She was right. There was no moon.
It had been there just a moment ago, surely, but now
the water had sucked it into its belly, swallowed it
whole. . . .

Suddenly Walter felt afraid. He had been afraid of
many things—thousands of things, it seemed to him
sometimes—but never of the Gulf, never before. He had
been born with its sound in his ears, its taste on his
tongue; its murmur had lulled him to sleep in his cradle
—how could he fear it? But tonight it was unfamiliar, a
living, breathing thing—a dark animal that sighed and
rushed at him, as if it wanted to gobble him up, then
changed its mind at the last second and retreated, only
to rush at him again. . . .

"Devil gonna come crawlin' outa the Gulf again someday—carry ever'body off this time—old fool, too . . . ,"
he whispered.

"Walter, you're scarin' me. Let's go back, Walter,"
Alice pleaded.

"Just a minute, Sister." His teeth were chattering, though the wind was warm. "Just a minute—" He heaved back his good arm and with all his might flung first the driftwood, then the beads, as far as he could— out into the water, out into the rushing, tumbling waves.

"All right, then!" he shouted. "I'm finished with you, you hear me?"

The water surged around his feet. It was icy cold against his hot skin.

Alice took his hand, tugged at it gently. "Come *on*, Walter."

This time he didn't resist. He was too tired. "Finished," he sighed, shuddering.

BOOK TWO

The floods have lifted up, O Lord,
the floods have lifted up their voice;
the floods lift up their waves.

—PSALM *93:3*

• Chapter 13

The fever lasted for five days. Mama had to be told of it, and though Walter cussed Alice for telling, his mother was grateful to have him need her, as he was glad to have her cool hands on his hot head, glad to be fed and fussed over as if he were a baby. Little by little the ache inside him began to ease. August slipped quietly into September, each day a hairsbreadth shorter than the one before. Goldenrod glowed at the edge of the melon fields.

The first Friday of September dawned bright as an angel's smile. Walter awoke with the early morning light. He lay still for a few minutes, trying to work his way through the cobwebs in his brain. He had had the oddest dream—something about a white crane, like the one he and Papa had seen that day on the way to the Landing. . . . What was it Mama had said a crane was supposed to mean—good luck flying south, bad for north? Or was it the other way around? Not that it really mattered. The crane in the dream hadn't flown anywhere; it was sitting on a nest of some kind—just sitting, staring at Walter. He had gone up close to it, and it hadn't been at all afraid. Suddenly it had begun to hoot like an owl, and then the hooting had turned to laughing, and the laughing had turned to crowing. . . . No, it wasn't the crane that was crowing; it was Sam Houston—good old Sam. Walter opened his eyes and stretched a mighty stretch.

"You feelin' all right, Walter?" Alice's brown eyes considered him anxiously. Even though he had been better for several days now, she still watched him every minute, fretting over him like a little old lady.

"I'm fine, Sister," said Walter. "Just fine—you don't have to worry so."

Alice looked doubtful. "How's your arm?"

"It's fine—just a tiny bit sore, that's all." Walter stretched it out and wiggled his fingers. "See there? Practically good as new."

She frowned at him. "Don't you ever get sick like that again, Walter Carroll. You like to scared me to death."

"Yes'm, Miss Alice."

"I'm not foolin', Walter!"

"Wah-wah," said Emily. She was standing up, smiling in the middle of her crib. "Wah-wah!"

"Why, look at Emily!" Alice cried. "She's not holdin' onto anything. Look, Walter!"

"I'm lookin'."

"Wah-wah," Emily said again. She took two steps with her arms outstretched, then clutched the side of the crib and beamed with pride.

Alice clapped her hands. "She walked, Walter—did

you see her? She took two steps all by herself! Hooray for Emily!"

"Ray!" cried Emily.

"Good for you, Emily!" said Walter, lifting her out of the crib and standing her up on her wobbly little legs in the middle of the floor. "Here, now, try it again—that's right—" Emily took three steps this time, then sat down hard on her bottom.

"Ray!" she crowed.

"Well, looka there, Alice—she's walkin' better'n you, now! See, I told you she'd learn to walk if you quit carryin' her around all over the place. Good thing for her you sprained your ankle!"

"Aw, it wasn't 'cause of that. She just wasn't ready before now, that's all. Come on, Emily, walk to Sister."

They walked her back and forth between them for a good while after that, laughing and hooraying and raising such a ruckus that their father and mother came in to see what was going on.

"Well, I'll declare—look at my baby girl walking!" Papa cried.

"My, my!" said Mama, and then the two of them sat right down on the floor with the children, and everyone laughed and exclaimed and applauded as Emily careened recklessly from one to the other. Walter couldn't remember the last time they had all been so happy together.

He swung the pail and whistled as he started out to tend to the milking; he had been up to doing light chores for a couple of days now. Lord, but he felt good. It was a perfect day—a little warmer than usual, maybe, but perfect all the same. The sky was pink as rose petals. The water was greenish blue, running at the beach in heady swells. Gulls wheeled above it, mewing like kittens. It felt to Walter as if some terrible curse had been lifted from the world, as if all creation had been made over, given a second chance. . . .

"That old man had us all half-crazy, Miz Long," he told her, leaning his head against her comfortable haunch as the milk squirted into the pail. "But that's over now, ain't it?"

Papa was dressed in his Sunday best by the time Walter came back inside. He had seen another load of melons off in the Barretts' boat yesterday; today he was bound for Galveston again. "I wish I could take you with me, son," he said. "I know it's been a long time since you had a holiday, but your mother thinks it's too soon after your fever for you to go traveling."

"I don't mind, Papa." It was the truth. Nothing could bother Walter today. "I can stay here and keep an eye on things while you're gone."

"I'd appreciate that, son."

They took the wagon over to the depot again. Alice and Emily sat up in front with Papa. Walter stretched out in back with his hands behind his head, enjoying the feel of the sun on his skin, only half-listening to Alice's chatter as the wagon bumped along on the sand. . . .

"Audie Merle's baby brother is nearly eighteen months old and he's not walkin' yet—d'you know that, Papa? And Emily's still two weeks shy of a year! Mama says early walkin's a sign of superior intelligence, and every one of us was early. She says William and me both walked when we were just ten months, and Walter walked at nine. I guess that makes him the smartest, but I don't know, he says he never could do arithmetic worth a flip."

Little Emily pointed at a cow. "Dog," she said, quite plainly.

"No, Emily," Alice laughed, "that's an old moo-cow. Say mooo-cow . . . mooooo-cow . . ."

"Dog," said Emily.

Alice collapsed in giggles. "Aw, come on, Emily, say moo-cow. You're s'posed to be smart!"

"Dog," Emily insisted, and everybody laughed. It felt so good to laugh again. . . .

Once they saw Papa off on the Gulf & Interstate, the children took their time going home. Walter held up Dowling for a while and let Emily sit in his lap, while Alice climbed out of the wagon and picked wildflowers for their mother—black-eyed Susans and bottle brushes and butterflyweed and great flaming tufts of goldenrod.

"Well, aren't they lovely!" Mama exclaimed when they put them in her hands. She looked so pretty standing there smiling, with the flowers lighting up her face, that on a sudden impulse Walter grabbed her waist and spun her around the kitchen.

"Merciful heavens! Stop that, Walter—you're going to break both our necks!" Mama protested, but she didn't look all that displeased.

Alice was waltzing with Emily, too. "Don't stop, Mama! 'Member when you and Papa showed us how you used to dance?"

But Mama had pulled away from Walter and was leaning against the kitchen table, breathless, her cheeks flushed. She shook her head. "That was a long time ago, Sister."

"No, it wasn't—'member, Papa told 'bout the time he played like he was Episcopalian so he could dance with you at the All Saints Ball—don't you 'member, Mama? And you said he was the handsomest one in his sailor suit!"

Lillie Carroll turned her face away and pinned up a loose curl at the nape of her neck. "You children run along now," she murmured vaguely. "I've got to see to these preserves. . . ."

"Come on, Sister," said Walter. "Mama's busy." He wished to goodness Alice would have sense enough to keep her mouth closed just once.

WALTER AND ALICE walked out to the beach in the afternoon. Alice was hardly limping at all now. The sky had clouded over some time after dinner, and the water was rough. *Might be some rain later on,* Walter reflected. *Be good—cool things off a little.*

Alice dropped down on her knees and started pushing the sand in a pile. Walter walked on a way without her, then came back and watched. "What are you makin'?" he asked after a while.

"A house," said Alice. "Like the one I'm gonna have someday."

"Where you gonna get a house?"

"My husband'll build it for me," she said matter-of-factly.

"Your *husband?*" The idea of little old scrawny Alice with a husband was too much for Walter. "You got one picked out already?"

"Course not," Alice replied. "But it don't hurt to think ahead."

Walter hooted. "Don't tell me—it's Junior Johnson, right? Tell the truth, Alice, you gone on old Junior?"

"You just hush, Walter Carroll." Alice threw a handful of sand at her brother.

He laughed. "What's for supper tonight, Miz Johnson?"

"You better not call me that—" She held up another clump of sand in her fist. "I mean it, Walter!"

"All right, all right." Walter sat down and crossed his legs. This was too good to miss. "Come on, tell me about this house of yours."

Alice looked at him suspiciously. "Not if you're gonna laugh—"

"I won't laugh, I promise," said Walter, straightening out his face as best he could.

"Well, all right . . . Looka here—this is the parlor, and there's the kitchen, and right over there's the sleepin' porch."

"Why, it's just like our house."

"Mm-hmm . . . and here's where the stairs'll go, up to the second story."

"What's this stickin' up out here?"

"Those are my palm trees, two on each side of the house—see? And here's the kitchen garden. I'll have snap beans and tomatoes and such in back, and my flowers up front—love-in-a-mist and lobelia and pinks, just like Mama's."

"How many children you gonna have?"

"Four," Alice answered without hesitation. "Two boys and two girls."

"Well, that's just exactly like our family!" exclaimed
Walter. "Ain't you gonna have *anything* different?"

"No," Alice said firmly. Then she paused. " 'Cept—"

" 'Cept what?"

" 'Cept aren't any of my children ever gonna get sick
and die."

"Oh."

Walter picked up a lightning whelk and held it to
his ear. It was funny to hear the real ocean with one
ear and the ocean caught inside the shell with the
other. . . .

"Ain't it hot, though?" he said after a time, just to
say something.

Alice nodded. "Sure is. I'm sweatin' somethin'
terrible."

"Maybe it'll rain tonight, kinda clear the air. . . ."

"That'd be good." Alice began poking windows in
her sand house. "If it rains, let's go out to the barn and
tell ghost stories, like we did that other time. 'Member
that day, Walter? That was when you first told me 'bout
old Tom comin' back."

Walter remembered, all right. Lord, did he remember.

"I guess he wasn't really all them things we thought,
was he?" Alice said wistfully, when another moment had
passed.

"Naw," said Walter. He crossed his arms and stared
out at the water. The waves were ugly brown now,
full of sand. They sounded like thunder, crashing on
the beach. "Naw, he wasn't nothin' but a crazy old
man. . . ." Walter didn't want to think about Tom
anymore. "Come on, Sister," he said suddenly, jumping
up. "I'll race you to the sand hills."

· · ·

RICHARD CARROLL took one last bite of Mary Agnes's lemon mystery pudding and leaned back from the crowded dinner table at the home of his Galveston relatives. He was doing his best—and failing—to follow the convoluted course of Cousin Jack Carroll's latest anecdote.

"So you see, Richard, the point is, if she really wanted to marry him, she ought to have stayed home!" Laughter shook Cousin Jack's big frame from his head to his toes and sent tears streaming down his broad, pink face. "Ought to have stayed home!" he repeated, giggling helplessly, "stayed *home!*" Cousin Jack roared with laughter, screamed with laughter, wiped his eyes and composed himself, then collapsed again, convulsed.

Richard laughed too, not so much at the story, of which he could make neither head nor tail, but because it was impossible to resist Cousin Jack's all-embracing merriment.

Mary Agnes smiled dimly; she never understood her husband's jokes either. "Well, if you gentlemen will excuse me, I believe it's time to put these children down for their nap. Come along, K.K., Bussy; you, too, little Jack. Now, Richard, you just make yourself right at home."

He stood up. "Thank you for your hospitality, Mary Agnes—and that dinner! I believe it was the best yet."

"You flatter me," Mary Agnes replied, coloring a little. "We all know what a famous cook Lillie is. My fried chicken could never hold a candle to hers."

"Now, I wouldn't say that," said Richard, though it was the truth.

"Well," said Mary Agnes, disentangling a twin from her skirts, "I do hope we can count on you for supper. You'll be staying the night, won't you?"

"If it won't be putting you to too much trouble. I do still have some business to attend to this afternoon. The fellow I generally see at the bank wasn't in his office this morning."

"No trouble atall," Cousin Jack interjected heartily. "No sense in you trying to rush back to Bolivar this evening. You can go back tomorrow just as well." He began to chuckle again. "Ought to have stayed home— tell the truth, Richard, isn't that just about the funniest thing you ever heard? Ought to have stayed home. . . ."

The gentleman was still out of his office when Richard arrived back at the bank. Being in no particular hurry, he passed the time quite pleasantly reading a copy of *The Galveston Daily News* that he'd picked up on his way. It was mostly devoted to stories about the current presidential race, which he had been following with interest; he was a William Jennings Bryan man himself. When he had read enough to decide afresh that the *News* was making a boneheaded blunder in backing McKinley again, he turned to the weather report on page 8. It had occurred to him that he ought to have a look at the forecast; his barge crossing had been a trifle choppy. If there was rough weather due, he still had time to catch the evening train back home. Storms unnerved Lillie so; he didn't like to be away if there was any chance of one. But the outlook for today was reassuring—"partly cloudy, with showers and cooler on the coast." Cooler—that would be a welcome change. . . . He adjusted the stiff collar that was sticking to his neck. . . . For tomorrow, Saturday, "fair, with fresh, possibly brisk northerly winds on the coast."

Just below the weather report another article mentioned "a tropical storm . . . centered over southern Florida and moving slowly northward. . . ." Nothing for Texas to worry about. Besides, Richard had seen the sunrise that morning—just the faintest blush of pink—nowhere near a sailor's warning red. So there was no need to hurry home. That was good; there were a couple of boats he had been intending to take a look at in the morning. High time he owned his own boat. He smiled to think how pleased Walter would be. . . .

The waiting room seemed unusually stuffy. Richard stood up and removed his coat. He was just hanging it carefully on the back of his chair when the secretary appeared.

"Mr. Arnoult will see you now," he announced, then shook his head sympathetically as Richard began putting his coat back on. "Hot as Hades, isn't it?"

"That it is," Richard agreed. "But I understand it's supposed to cool off later on this evening."

"Glad to hear it," said the secretary, holding the door open for him.

LILLIE CARROLL sat beside the crib on the sleeping porch, fanning the baby. It was too hot to sleep. The sun had long since set, but the clouds that stretched from horizon to horizon held in the heat, pushed it at the earth like an old wool blanket. Emily was fretful with it. Her yellow curls clung damply to her head, her cheeks were as rosy as if she'd run a mile.

Lillie's wrist ached. She transferred the straw fan to

her other hand. Lord, it was a ragged old souvenir. Richard had brought it to her from Brazil when they were courting—what was it?—fifteen years ago? More like fifteen hundred, it seemed, sometimes. . . .

The fan was painted with faded colors that had once been bright—yellow birds and blue birds and red roses and green leaves—all of them surrounding a gaily dressed señorita who held out her hand to a kneeling, mustachioed señor . . . *a silly, sentimental picture,* Lillie thought now, but once it had given her pleasure. . . .

Emily closed her eyes and put her thumb in her mouth. Lillie reached over and tried gently to remove it, but the little girl whimpered and wouldn't let go. *Well, never mind.* Lillie was too tired to fight about it; surely one more night of thumb-sucking wouldn't ruin the child's mouth forever. *William had a beautiful mouth, though he sucked two fingers for the longest time.* . . .

She sighed. *Strange it's still so hot, with the Gulf as rough as it was this afternoon.* . . . Usually big waves meant a stiff wind blowing in off the water, but what wind there had been today had come in gusts from the north, and that had brought little relief. The Carroll house wasn't built to welcome the north wind.

Lillie's eyes traveled to her two older children. Walter and Alice lay quietly in their beds, their eyes closed. *Gracious, Walter's getting big! His toes nearly touch the foot of his bed now. He must have grown a head taller this summer. He's his father's son, all right, no question about that. Just as William was mine.* . . . The old ache rose in her throat. Lord, she missed him so. Sometimes she felt as if she just couldn't stand it any longer. But she had to stand it, didn't she? There was nothing else she could do. She had prayed to God to let her die too, but it hadn't done any good. "His ways are not our ways, Sister Carroll," Dr. Croombs had told her after Emily's birth. "We can only thank Him for sending another healthy child to take the place of the one He has called. . . ." *Take his place! As if anyone could ever take William's place!* Lillie had had to bite her tongue to keep from calling the old man a fool; he was only trying to help, after all.

"God's ways are not our ways. . . ." *Well, that, at least, is the truth.* As Lillie saw it, the only real mystery was that anyone still cared for a God with such ways. . . .

My, but it's warm. Lillie was perspiring, and she seldom perspired. Alice must have dropped off; her breathing was slow, regular. Lillie's eyes rested on the soft, almost babyish curve of her jaw, the stubborn chin relaxed in sleep. She looked so vulnerable just now. They all did—even Walter, big as he was. . . .

A change of light drew her eyes to the window. Through a rent in the clouds, the moon was shining, bright as day nearly, and just a cat's whisker away from being full. Then the clouds closed again, and she looked away. To see the moon darkened was never a good omen. . . .

Emily was asleep at last, her thumb still clamped in her puckered lips. Lillie rose quietly from her rocking chair and started across the room.

" 'Night, Mama."

The sound of Walter's voice startled her. *He's been awake all this time, then?*

"Good night, son," she said.

TOM SAT ALONE in the small jail at High Island, listening to the faraway roar of the surf. *It's comin',* he told himself. *Old Gulf's comin' for Tom, ain't it? Been waitin' for me all this time, now it thinks it's gonna get me. . . . Cain't tell, though. Fooled the devil this long, maybe I's gonna fool him again . . . cain't tell, cain't tell. . . .*

He stood up and began to pace around his cell. He was stiff from sitting still so long. He was eighty-two years old, but his muscles might have belonged to a strong man half his age; they were that lean and hard. It was only sitting still that made him tired.

They had given him a cot for sleeping, but he never slept on it; it would have caused him no end of grief to spend the night trying not to roll off its narrow limits. Now he stood precariously on it instead and looked out the one tiny window. The moon struggled out from behind the clouds and stared, then hid again. Tom pointed at it. "That's right—you best stay away from here," he said aloud, "if you got any sense. . . ."

A sudden gust of wind snaked in over his head and fluttered the leaves of the illustrated Bible Mrs. Leola Sparks had left open on the three-legged table beside the cot. It had once been a four-legged table, but it got by on three these days. . . . Tom put his head to one side and listened. *Wind's changin'. New sound in it now,*

*kinda whinin', cryin' like cats. No other sound just the
same. . . . Flood tide be startin' 'fore mornin'. . . .*

He climbed down from the cot and looked at the
picture the wind had turned up in the Bible. An old
man with a long white beard was riding through the
sky in a funny-looking wagon all afire. That wasn't so
bad by itself, but the poor horses pulling the wagon
looked like they were burning up too. Some mighty
unusual things in that book. . . .

Mrs. Sparks had taken it upon herself to reform him.
She visited twice a week to read aloud out of the Bible,
then lecture him at length about the error of his ways.
And she generally felt called upon to finish up with a
hymn. Tom didn't mind her talk so much; he could
pretty well fix his head so the words just flowed in one
ear and out the other without doing much damage. Her
singing, now—that was something else again. As close
as he could make out, it took from Friday till Tuesday
for his head to stop ringing. But the lady had a good
heart, which Tom appreciated. She also baked a mean
peach pie, which he appreciated even more.

The sheriff's wife was a pretty fair cook herself; for
the first time in years Tom was threatening to get some
meat on his bones. It was only being cooped up he
minded—cooped up just like one of those old chickens
he had set free three weeks back. They hadn't liked
being cooped up either; Tom had seen that about them
right off and had eaten them purely as an act of kindness.

The wind whistled in again through the window. He
lifted his head and sniffed it. *Don't smell right*, he told
himself. *It's comin'. I know it's comin'. . . .*

But he was comparatively safe here on High Island. It wasn't really an island at all, just so called because the salt dome it sat on lifted the settlement up so high above the surrounding country that in bad storms it looked like an island rising from the flooded plains. It was the people in Galveston and down on the rest of the peninsula who ought to be worrying. *Them chirren that b'long to that melon farm and that little brown dog—they in plenty trouble. Missy and that boy— Walter, he say his name was. Course maybe they folks got sense 'nough to get outa there in time. . . .*

There was a sudden rattling, clicking noise, and Tom looked up through the bars of his cell to see the front door of the jailhouse swinging open. Lester Barrett walked inside. Either he or Sheriff Elliott looked in on Tom last thing every night to make sure High Island's one and only prisoner was locked up safe and sound.

"Hey, Tom, what you know good?"

"Not a whole lot. Had that Christian lady come 'round here again today—that's 'bout all. She say look like I's goin' to hell slicker'n a greased goose."

Lester chuckled. He was a mite red about the eyes. Tom judged he'd raised a glass or two this evening. "Miz Sparks is one heck of a Christian, that's for sure. But if she's been botherin' you, Tom, you ought to've told us. The sheriff could've asked her not to come anymore."

"Naw, she ain't botherin' me none. She can talk 'bout Jesus all she want, long as she keep bringin' them pies." Tom raised his eyebrows. "But I'd sure be grateful if you could figger some way to keep her from singin'."

Lester laughed out loud. Tom always made him laugh.

"There's folks at church been tryin' to figger how to do that for twenty years or more, Tom. Might just as well tell the wind not to blow."

"Couldn't do that tonight," Tom muttered, glancing behind him at the window.

"What say?" asked Lester, pulling up a chair just outside Tom's cell and making himself comfortable. He often liked to stay and visit a little. There was never any telling what Tom would say—might make for a good story later on. . . .

"Talkin' 'bout the wind, that's all," said Tom. "Smell like a storm comin'."

"Naw, Tom—I saw the *News* today. May be a shower tonight, that's all; they're lookin' for blue skies tomorrow."

Tom snorted. "They can look all they want—they ain't gonna find 'em. Devil storm comin' sure as I's sittin' here. Folks got any sense, they be long gone 'fore tomorrow."

Lester frowned. "Aw, c'mon, Tom, you're givin' me the creepin' willies. Seems to me you ought to be in a good mood tonight. I got a surprise for you."

Tom looked suspicious. "What kinda surprise?"

Lester winked. "I've just come from supper over't the sheriff's house. He thinks you've learned your lesson—says we can turn you loose first thing in the mornin'."

Tom sat up straight. "That right?"

"That's right—under one condition. Sheriff says you got to promise to move on right away. He doesn't want Rupert Bland or anybody else gettin' riled up all over again. You show your face on this peninsula, you gonna find yourself in serious trouble. There's people in Galveston can see to it you're locked up for good, you hear me?" Lester looked serious now.

"I hear you."

"You understand this is the sheriff talkin', don't you, Tom? Personally, I got nothin' against you. . . ."

"I understand."

"Well, that's fine, then. . . ." Lester got to his feet. He was suddenly feeling ill at ease. There was something in Tom's steady gaze that he had never seen before—something hard, unyielding. This wasn't the Tom that always made him laugh. . . . "I'll, uh, I guess I'll say good night, now. . . ."

" 'Scuse me, uh, deputy—"

Lester was already halfway out the door. He turned around. "What is it, Tom?"

"I was just thinkin'— If it's all the same to you, you s'pose they's any way you could turn me loose tonight?"

"Tonight? Don't seem like that'd make much sense, Tom—turnin' you out in the dark. Never heard of such a thing. You best get a good night's sleep while you can. I doubt you'll have a bed comfortable as this tomorrow."

Tom eyed the narrow cot. "Not likely . . ."

Lester turned to go again.

"Uh, deputy—"

Lester paused. "Yes?"

"Seem like I cain't breathe so good, cooped up."

Lester shook his head. "You know I cain't let you go on my own, Tom. Sheriff'd have my hide."

Tom didn't say anything. He only looked at Lester with a look that Walter knew, and Alice knew, and Crockett understood. . . .

A minute passed. Two minutes. Lester rubbed his

jaw and shifted uncomfortably. He had had too much of Mrs. D. L. Elliott's best blackberry wine at supper. His head was beginning to ache. "Well," he said at last, "guess it wouldn't hurt—long as you promise to stay out of trouble. . . ."

"I ain't goin' near it."

"Well, all right, then . . . s'pose I ought to have my head examined, but it don't really seem like a few hours could make much difference, one way or t'other."

Minutes later the two of them were standing outside the jail. Lester handed Tom his old shovel and the gunnysack. "I b'lieve these are yours."

"B'lieve so."

Lightning flashed somewhere far out at sea. Tom counted all the fingers on one hand and two on the other. There was the sound of distant thunder.

"Looks like you might be right 'bout that storm, after all," said Lester. His head was splitting now. "But ten to one it'll blow over 'fore sunrise."

"Don't you count on it," said Tom. "You just stick up here on high ground—that's your best bet 'gainst the devil."

Lester laughed nervously. "I'll remember that, Tom. You take it easy now."

"You too, Mr. Deputy."

He walked off into the darkness.

• Chapter 14

Walter—wake up, Walter! Look outside!"

Walter groaned and turned over on his back. Alice's face hung over him like a small, pale moon. Her brown eyes looked black in the gray morning light, shiny as polished buttons.

"What is it, Sister?" He was so tired. It had taken him such a long time to fall asleep in the heat, and then he had slept fitfully, drifting in and out of dreams that had no shape or sense. . . .

"Just look out there, Walter. I never seen such big waves, did you?"

He sat up and looked out the window. "Hell's bells," he murmured, his heart in his mouth.

The beach had all but disappeared. Almost all the way to the railroad tracks there were huge, gray waves, leaping up high as mountains, crashing into each other like battling elephants.

"Did you ever see the water come so far in, Walter? I know I never did!" Alice sounded more excited than scared.

Walter shook his head. He couldn't speak; it felt as if his tongue were glued to the roof of his mouth. He had never actually seen a bad Gulf overflow himself, but he had heard stories—terrible stories. The whole town of Indianola, washed clean away back in '86 . . . houses blown to kingdom come . . . men, women, children, sucked right up, never to be seen again. Walter stared out at the angry water and thought again of that night on the beach—his sudden fear that the Gulf was a dark animal, waiting to pounce. . . .

Alice snuggled up next to him. "You think it could come in as far as our house?"

Walter shook his head again. *Surely the water couldn't come in that far,* he told himself. *It's never come that far before. . . .*

"I guess not," Alice agreed. She sounded disappointed. "But I'm glad Papa built our house up so high, just in case."

Emily opened her eyes and smiled. She stood up in her crib and held out her hands to Alice.

"Hey there, baby girl," Alice said, lifting her out and bringing her over to Walter's bed. "You want to see some big old waves?"

"Bye-bye," said Emily, waving her chubby hand at the water.

"No, Emily," Alice laughed, "not wave bye-bye— *waves.* Water waves—see?"

"See," said Emily, beaming happily. "See, bye-bye!"

"No, no—oh, Emily . . ." Alice fell down laughing. Emily climbed into Walter's lap.

"For cryin' out loud, Alice, she's soppin' wet!" he

cried, finding his voice at last. "Get her off me, will you?"

"Well, all right. You don't have to get so mad."

"I'm not mad," said Walter, but he was. He was mad because he was scared. How come he couldn't be like his sisters and not know enough to be scared?

"Doesn't seem like the wind's blowin' all that hard, does it?" said Alice, as she pinned fresh diapers on the baby. "Funny sound to it, though—can you hear it?"

Walter could hear it, all right. It sounded like nothing he had ever heard before—keening, dismal, as if everyone who had ever died had waited till now to complain about it. "It's awful," he murmured.

"Well, least it's not hot anymore," Alice said cheerfully. "Fact, it's goin' on cold, I'd say."

"I thought I heard voices—you all up?" Mama stood in the doorway, wrapped in the quilt from her bed. She looked agitated.

"Yes'm, we're up," said Alice. "Did you see them giant waves, Mama?"

"*Those* waves," Lillie corrected her automatically, absently, as if her heart weren't really in it. "Yes, I saw them, all right. Looks like we're in for a storm," she went on, pulling the quilt closer about her. "You'd better tend to the milking right away, Walter, before the rain gets started. Alice, you mind the baby while I get these windows closed."

In his worry Walter had forgotten all about Jane Long, but now he jumped from bed, glad to have something to do.

Crockett came running as soon as he stepped out the

front door. He looked alert, frisky as a puppy. He put his front paws on Walter's chest and licked his chin.

"Hey, boy, you're in a good mood this mornin'. Come on, now, get down. I got work to do. You like storms, too—that it? You crazy like Alice?"

Crockett barked happily and bounded about, wagging his tail.

"I guess that's it, all right," said Walter, scratching him behind the ears. "Dumb dog." He shook his head disapprovingly, but a part of him understood. Out here, with the wind whipping his hair in his eyes and the surf thundering in his ears, he felt a kind of fearful exhilaration himself, as if he might sprout wings and fly any second, borne on the wind as lightly as a hen feather. . . . *Well, it's only a storm, after all—nothing to get all worked up over.* So what if they did have a little overflow? Papa had built the house up plenty high, just like Alice said. Best-built house on the whole peninsula—strong and safe as Papa's own arms. There was no need to worry. None at all. Walter took a deep breath of the salty air and squared his shoulders. He was all right now.

Jane Long was standing patiently by the barn door, waiting for him to let her inside. She had heeded the peculiar sound in the wind, too. Even dumb old Dowling had come in from the pasture. He fixed Walter with a wall-eyed stare, then went back to cropping grass, his ears twitching nervously back and forth while he chewed. Above the yowling of the wind Walter could hear Sam Houston and his wives cackling and fretting in the henhouse.

"What's everybody so nervous for?" Walter frowned at the animals as he opened the barn door. "Just a storm, that's all. We've had storms before, ain't we?"

At that moment Crockett gave two short barks and went tearing past Walter's knees and out into the melon field.

"Well, what's got into him?" Walter said aloud, and then he saw. There was someone out there—a man, getting closer now—carrying something on his shoulder —a shovel, it looked like. . . .

Oh, Lord, it cain't be. It just cain't be. . . .

It was. Tom the Tramp, old Tom himself, big as life. Crockett was already at his side, licking his hand.

Walter stood rooted to the spot, watching him come.

"No SENSE you lookin' like that," said Tom. "I ain't no ghost."

"I thought . . . I thought . . ." Walter stammered.

"You think too much, boy. Get you in trouble ever' time."

"But . . . they put you in jail."

The old man closed one eye. "Ain't no jail can hold Tom for long."

"You broke out?"

He shrugged. "Got no time to stand 'round talkin'. Devil storm already started—cain't you see? Y'all got to get outa here 'fore it's too late."

A shudder ran through Walter's body. In his mind's eye, the dark animal tensed its muscles, poised itself to spring. . . . He shook the thought loose. He had had enough of Tom's crazy talk to last a lifetime—two lifetimes. He wasn't going to start listening to it again now. "We ain't goin' anyplace. My papa knows all about storms. He built our house plenty strong."

Tom snorted. "Ain't no house that strong, boy. I was born in a herrycane, s'posed to die in one someday— guess I know. You let me talk to your papa."

"You cain't. He's in Galveston," Walter said, and then he flushed. Maybe it wasn't such a good idea to say that his father was gone. He drew himself up as tall as he could. "You can talk to me. I'm the one in charge."

Tom narrowed his eyes. "You chirren here by your-self? Ain't your mama home?"

Walter wasn't about to let Tom frighten his mother. "Mama don't want to talk to you. You stay away from her, you hear me? Just leave her alone. Leave us all alone—"

"How old are you, boy?" Tom interrupted him.

"Thirteen," said Walter.

"You want to make fourteen, you best listen." Tom pointed a gnarled finger at him. "Ain't nothin' gonna be alive where we standin', this time tomorrow. You tell your mama that."

Walter stuck out his chin. "I told you—I'm the one in charge. You better go on now."

Tom regarded the boy calmly for a moment. Then he turned around and started to walk away.

Walter watched him go. A whole summerful of warring emotions struggled in his stomach. "Wait!" he cried suddenly; the word tore loose from his throat in a strangulated howl before he could stop it.

Tom turned around. "You talkin' to me?"

"Why'd you come back here, anyway? If anybody sees you, they just gonna lock you up again."

To his surprise, Tom grinned. "Ain't nobody ever told you I's crazy, boy?" He had to shout it over the wind. "You warned me one time, now I warned you. Go on—milk your cow. She gonna have trouble enough 'fore this day's over."

THE RAIN began to fall while Walter was still in the barn. It plunked on the tin roof in heavy drops, sporadic at first—two, three, a scant half-dozen—then suddenly a thousand at once, till Walter was deaf with the sound of them. Water was coming down in cataracts by the time he got back to the house, lugging the pailful of milk.

All during breakfast Alice kept jumping up from the table to run to the window and check on the progress of the waves.

"Ooh, Mama, they're right up against the railroad tracks now. . . . I'll declare, you shoulda seen the size of that one. I bet it was ten times tall as Papa! You reckon the fishes are gettin' seasick, swirlin' 'round like that? I know I would be."

"Alice, I don't care to hear any more about that awful water, and besides, your breakfast is getting stone cold," Mama chided, as she put a spoonful of milk toast in Emily's mouth. "Now, you come sit down at your place and stay there till you're done—you know better."

"Yes, ma'am." Alice slid into her chair, but she was too excited to eat. Her eyes kept darting toward the window.

Walter didn't feel much like eating, himself; his stomach was still tangled up in knots from Tom's visit. Surely he had done the right thing, said what Papa would have wanted him to say—surely he had. . . . But he didn't *feel* sure. . . . *For cryin' out loud, why cain't I ever feel sure of anything?*

"Walter, you've hardly touched your cheese grits," Mama said, "and I thought they were your favorite!"

"Yes, ma'am, they are. They're real good. I'm just— not too hungry. . . ."

"You're not feeling feverish again, are you?" His mother put her hand to his forehead.

He pulled away in exasperation. "No, ma'am, I feel just *fine.*"

"Well, there's no need to snap at me," Mama said in a strained voice; then, more gently, "I expect it's just this weather has you upset. I don't wonder, with your father still off visiting those relatives of his. I tell you what—I'll make boiled custard later on. My mother always said there's nothing like boiled custard to soothe the nerves."

"Mama," Walter said suddenly, "do you s'pose we ought to take the wagon over to High Island 'fore this storm gets any worse?"

"Goodness, no, Walter—just look at that rain! Why, we'd be drenched! I don't see what good it would do us, anyway. You know your father insists we're perfectly safe in a storm as long as we stay in this house, and I s'pose we have to trust he knows what he's talking about. I expect this old wind's going to blow itself out before long, anyhow."

"I expect so. . . ." said Walter, staring disconsolately into his bowl. It was true—Papa had said it, and, of course, he knew. He had been a sailor; he knew all about those things, Walter told himself. But here came the memory of Tom's voice, whispering in his other ear: *Ain't nothin' gonna be alive where we're standin', this time tomorrow. . . .*

Lightning flashed. Thunder rolled.

"I do wish your father would get here," Mama said, glancing nervously out the window. "Surely he knows to come straight home; I can't believe he'd fool around in Galveston looking at boats in wheather like this! But then, I s'pose you never can figure what a man will do. You know what my papa used to say to me? 'Daughter', he'd say, 'all men are sorry, but some are sorrier than others.' If he said it once, he said it a thousand times."

"He'll come," said Walter. He had never wanted his father so much in his life. "I bet he's on his way back right this minute."

"No, sir, no trains that way this morning. Barge can't cross for a while, not till this storm passes, anyhow." The man at the ticket office was polite but firm.

An irritated muscle twitched in Richard's jaw. "Well, how'm I s'posed to get back to Bolivar, then?"

"I don't know, Mister. I don't guess you can," the man said patiently, then added with a chuckle, " 'less you're a better swimmer than I am."

Richard didn't laugh. "My family's over there by themselves," he said, frowning.

"Sorry, didn't mean to offend," said the man. "But I wouldn't worry. These things don't usually amount to much."

Richard nodded curtly, walked away from the window, and sat down on one of the waiting room benches;

they were sparsely filled with other would-be passengers.

"Ought to have stayed home," he said to himself under his breath. The line from his cousin's joke had run senselessly through his head since yesterday—only now did its meaning seem clear. He stood up again and took off his coat. It was wet through. He had had to walk quite a way in the rain. The streets close to the beach were flooded, so the trolleys weren't running. He had passed dozens of people who appeared to be in holiday mood, going down to see the huge breakers tumbling in, leaping up sky-high as they dashed against the pleasure piers. Galveston was full of folks who relished rough weather.

But Richard wasn't among them. He didn't like the looks of this storm. He didn't like the whining he had heard in the wind even before he had opened his eyes that morning. Not that it was blowing all that hard, but there was a peculiar sound in it that he had heard before in his days at sea, a sound that made sailors turn pale and cross themselves.

"Stay here till it blows over," Cousin Jack had told him at breakfast, but Richard had said no, he ought to be getting home; Lillie and the children would be wanting him there.

"Dang weather," he muttered now, as he settled himself against the hard wooden bench.

"I reckon it'll be over 'fore long," said a genial-looking white-haired man sitting nearby. "I've seen storms a lot worse than this. Biggest overflow they ever had here was in seventy-five—didn't do much more than make a mess."

"Yes, sir, I'm sure you're right," Richard said. "But

I'd really like to get on home. My wife doesn't like it much when I'm gone in bad weather."

The old man nodded understandingly. "High-strung type?"

"Yes, sir, I guess you could say that." Richard cleared his throat uncomfortably and looked down at his good shoes. They were caked with mud. "Course there's no reason for her to be nervous; our house is set up plenty high. Built it myself—solid as a rock, that house."

"Is that right?" The man looked impressed. "Where is it you live?"

"Over on Bolivar, 'bout mid-way between Flake and Rollover."

The man nodded again. "Well, sure, I know right where that is. Good melon country over there, isn't it?"

"Yes, sir, best in the world. I'm a melon farmer myself. Carroll's the name," he said, extending his hand.

"Pleased to meet you, Mr. Carroll," said the man, shaking it. "Milam, here, from Beaumont." There was a moment's quiet; then he spoke again. "You know, I've always wondered why they call it Rollover."

Richard chuckled. "That's an old story. Peninsula's so narrow there, they say that pirates used to roll barrels of rum from the Gulf over to East Bay—rolled 'em over, you see? Stayed clear of customs that way."

"Is that so? Old Lafitte, hmm?"

"Well, that's what they say. Folks claim he was all over the peninsula, but I don't know—sure wouldn't guess it from lookin' at it now. Bolivar's pretty tame, these days." He paused and shook his head. "Course, I got a boy still thinks he can find a pirate under every seashell."

Mr. Milam laughed. "I know what you mean. Raised a pair of boys myself."

The door blew open just then, letting in a gust of wind and rain and a couple of bedraggled-looking men.

"How's it lookin' out there?" Mr. Milam called out.

"Not too bad," one of the new arrivals answered. "Wind's not that much to speak of—got a little high water, that's all."

"How 'bout the bay?" Richard asked. "You think a good sailor could make it across to Bolivar?" It occurred to him that he might find somebody with a boat, pay him for his trouble. . . .

"Not a chance right now," said the other man. "Got some mighty big waves out there yet. But they ought to die down in an hour or two—always do. I'm bettin' it'll be over by noon."

Noon. Well, maybe so, thought Richard. *Maybe so* . . . There was nothing for it but to wait, now. He shifted around a little on the bench and did his best to make himself comfortable. "Ought to have stayed home," he sighed, for the hundredth time that morning.

"LOOKA THERE, Mama!" cried Alice, who had spent most of the morning with her nose pressed against the window. "Here comes the train!"

Sure enough, the Gulf & Interstate was chugging along through the driving rain, going a little slower than usual because of the water that was lapping against the tracks, but there it was—almost as solid and dependable as Papa himself. It would go to Galveston, after all, and bring him home—Walter was sure of it.

For the first time that day Mama smiled. "Well, that's a sight for sore eyes, she said. "Those train men know their business; they wouldn't be out there if there was. any real danger. I wouldn't be surprised if the worst was over now."

Walter looked at the grandfather clock: ten thirty. By a quarter of eleven, the Gulf had swallowed the beach whole, tracks and all, and was chewing on the sand hills. Walter saw it and turned anxiously to his mother.

"Mama, maybe we really ought to leave now. I could hitch up Dowling. We could try to make it to High Island before the water rises any more."

"Don't be ridiculous, Walter," his mother said sharply. "The roads will be nothing but mud after all this rain. The wagon'd be stuck in two minutes. Use your head, child!"

Walter hadn't thought of that. "Yes'm, I guess you're right," he said, doing his best to swallow the fear that was rising in him by the minute, threatening to choke him altogether. Mama was right to call him "child." It shamed him to think of it.

She took his hand apologetically. "There, son, I'm sorry to scold so. It's just this storm has my nerves stretched tight, that's all. Let's not have any more talk of leaving the house, shall we? I'm sure we're perfectly safe here. Why, I wouldn't go out in that rain for any-thing—you know how I dislike the water. I'm just like my papa that way; he used to say water would be fine if it just weren't so wet."

Now Walter had another worry to add to his list. *Lord,* he thought, *Mama cain't swim a lick. And Alice isn't much better; in a way, she's worse, since she hasn't got sense enough to be afraid.*

Please, God, he prayed, *don't let the water get any closer; I don't know if I can take care of 'em all by myself . . . please, God. . . .* He wished now that he had paid better attention to Dr. Croombs's boring sermons. Maybe there were secrets in them he had missed—magic words that would make the Almighty pay attention. "Please, God, please, God," he murmured over and over. It was the best he could do.

"I just can't believe your father's not back yet," Mama said. She sounded more irritated than anything else. "He's bound to know we're worried."

"Aw, ding-bust it!" Alice cried suddenly. She was still standing at the window, peering out at the water.

"Now, Sister, there's no use getting upset," Mama told her. "Walter's probably right. Papa's most likely on his way home right now."

"No, ma'am, it ain't that—"

"Isn't that."

"Isn't that," Alice repeated despondently.

"Well, what is it, then?"

"It's my sand house." Alice's voice trembled. "I guess it's ruint."

"For cryin' out loud," Walter muttered.

"Well, I'll just have to build another one tomorrow, that's all," Alice sighed. "You all think the water'll be back down by tomorrow?"

"Certainly it will," Mama said firmly.

"Well, sure," said Walter, hoping he sounded more confident than he felt. *Please, God, please, God. . . .*

• Chapter 15

The wind was growing stronger by the minute. Tom got so tired of trying to hold his old hat on his head that he finally took it off and stuffed it in the gunnysack. Rain was sharp against him, each drop a stinging needle, driven by the gale. Even his leathery old skin could feel its bite. Over his right shoulder he could see the Gulf, boiling like a stewpot over hellfire, inching closer with every wave.

For the fortieth time he stopped and looked behind him, to see if there was any sign of Walter and his family. . . . Nothing. *Well. Ain't no never mind to me,* Tom told himself. *I done warned 'em—nothin' else I could do. They want to get theyself kilt, that's they own business.*

He didn't really know why he had gone back in the first place—why he had ever thought they would listen to an old black man. Seemed like he just had to, some way. . . . It didn't matter, anyhow. All that mattered now was saving his own skin. Not that there were many would consider it a skin worth saving.

He walked on. The wind wanted to push him right off his feet, but he was too strong for it. Strong as an ox, even after all these years. . . .

"You ought to see this boy work a cane field," his master back in Louisiana had once bragged to a neighboring plantation owner. "He'd make five of your niggers, easy."

"Can he fight?" the other man had asked, looking Tom over critically from head to toe. "There's good money in a nigger that can fight."

"If I want him to," the master had answered. After that he had taught Tom to use his fists, to feint and punch and keep his guard up and punch again; and Tom had learned so well that the master had begun inviting his acquaintances to bring their black boys over for an evening's entertainment. Tom would fight them and beat them, and then the other owners would cuss, and money would change hands. "Worth his weight in gold," the master would exult. "I tell you, this boy's worth his weight in gold!" And to prove his point, when Tom had one of his front teeth cracked off by a man's knuckles and still came back and won the fight, the master took him to New Orleans and got him fitted up with a new tooth, made of solid gold. . . .

The Gulf looked closer than it had a minute ago. It would cover the whole peninsula before long, but Tom would be high and dry by then; he was halfway back to High Island now, nearly to Rollover. He had to get to Rollover in a hurry; that was the main thing. The land was so narrow there that the Gulf would sweep across it and meet the bay first chance it got, and then there would be no getting back to safety—too many low spots where the water would be deep and even a strong man couldn't fight it. . . .

He had hated the fighting—the headaches and bleeding noses and swollen eyes, the sickness he always felt when he saw the other man lying senseless at his feet. He thought a time or two of pretending he was no good, letting one of the others beat him, just to put an end to the whole business. But he was afraid the master would be angry and sell him, and he didn't want to be sold, not without his wife and his two little babies. He had married one of the house slaves, a fine-looking girl by the name of Alnetta. . . .

Alnetta. Even after all this time Tom could still see her laughing at him—making him laugh, too—just like it was yesterday. She was just a little bit of a thing, but Lord, she had a tongue on her, Alnetta did, the sharp-edged tip of a powerful temper. Crazy as he was about her, Tom sometimes had a hard time deciding which was more to be feared—the master's whip or Alnetta's tongue. But she was gentle as a lamb with her boy Louis and her little girl Evalina, loving them with a love so fierce that in the end it was that love, and not Tom's reluctance to fight, that caused all the trouble. . . .

Tom came to a gully where the waves were already breaking waist-high. He waded across and kept going, his body moving of its own accord through the water, his mind sixty years away, trapped in the languid heat of a late May afternoon, heavy with the lemony smell of magnolias. . . .

Alnetta had been minding the three children of the master's son, along with her own babies. A quarrel had started—a silly fight over a toy; one of the white children had accused Louis of trying to steal it. Before Alnetta had a chance to step between them, the white child, a big boy of seven or eight, knocked little Louis down and hit him hard. Alnetta promptly grabbed the white boy by the shoulders and shook him till his teeth rattled. Then she turned him over her knee and gave him a good spanking, to boot. The child broke away and ran to his mother, screaming bloody murder. . . .

A week later, while Tom was out working in the cane fields, Alnetta and the children were taken away and sold. Tom wasn't allowed to know where. He was kept, considered too valuable a piece of property to part with.

He tried to find them. He ran away from the plantation, but they caught him and brought him back. Then he refused to fight for his master, hoping, now, to be sold. He would stand like a rock in the middle of the ring and never raise a hand to defend himself, while his opponent's blows rained about his ears.

"What's the matter with your nigger?" the other owners would holler, and his master would cuss and threaten, but in vain. Tom would stand there unmoving, till at last he fell, mercifully unconscious. Disgusted, the master finally took him to New Orleans and sold him, but not to the people that had bought the rest of his family. His new master was a Georgia man by the name of Campbell. He was a kind man, in his way—at least he cared nothing for fighting. But Tom ran away from there too, and again they brought him back. Only this time he wasn't whipped; Mr. Campbell didn't believe in whipping his "nigras," as he called them. Instead, he spoke to Tom in a patient, fatherly sort of way.

"Haven't you been happy here, Tom? Aren't you treated well?"

Tom didn't answer.

"Come on, now, Tom. If you don't tell me what's wrong with you, there's no way I can help. Couldn't hurt to give me a chance, now, could it?"

Tom was sullen, suspicious. But his master was persistent, and after a while Tom told his story, since he had nowhere else to turn, no one else to trust. Campbell listened gravely—angrily at times, to Tom's surprise. Then he promised to do what he could to find what had become of Alnetta and the children, even to buy them himself if there was any chance of it at all. Tom was delirious with happiness and gratitude. For months he lived on tenterhooks, hoping against hope. . . .

He couldn't be more than a mile from Rollover now. It was hard to see in the driving rain, but he thought he could just make it out up ahead. He would be in time. He would make it through Rollover and back to High Island before the full fury of the storm was upon him. The wind roared in his ears, inside his head. . . .

Campbell had been as good as his word. He had made inquiries, written letters. Finally, he had set out on a business trip to New Orleans, promising Tom that he would continue the search during the course of his journey and bring Alnetta and the children back with him if he could.

"Put your trust in the Lord, Tom," he told him. "If it's His will that they be found, I'll find them."

Haltingly, only half-remembering how to do it, Tom prayed to Jesus. If he had to trust a white man, he reckoned he best pray to the white man's God. . . .

Campbell returned a month later.

Tom ran to meet him on the road, his heart nigh to bursting in his chest.

"I'm sorry, Tom." Campbell shook his head. "They're gone."

"Gone," Tom repeated softly. "Gone . . ." The word felt dead as it left his mouth.

"They were bought by a man from Texas, name of Hopkins. He and his family had just started growing sea island cotton on the Bolivar Peninsula, just across from Galveston. Seems there was a yellow fever epidemic over there in forty-four." Campbell's voice trailed off. Tom didn't say anything. Campbell cleared his throat, continued. "Looks like it got 'em all, Tom. Hopkins and his family too. I'm sorry."

Sorry. He was sorry. It didn't change anything. It didn't bring them back.

Tom stopped walking. He had made it to Rollover. The Gulf was still to his right but even closer now, lapping at his feet almost. The bay was scarcely more than a stone's throw to his left. The waters would meet in no time at all, dance their deadly dance, and that would be that.

One last time Tom turned, looked behind him through the curtain of rain. There was no one in sight. Those children and their mother—they must still be back at that house of theirs, just sitting there like white dummies, waiting for the old demon Gulf to come and sweep them away. Tom had warned them, but they hadn't listened, and now they would die, now they would be dead —dead as hammers, dead as nails, dead as Alnetta and Louis and Evalina. . . .

Well, what's it matter? Tom asked himself. *Ever'body got to die sooner or later. Might just as well be sooner— save 'em all a lot of trouble.*

Still . . . he wished he had never talked to them, never eaten their food, never watched the little girl's eyes get big when he told stories, that boy all the time trying to act like such a man. . . . Tom had never paid any mind to children before, not really, not since his own—except maybe to say boo and scare them off when they ran after him, hollering, throwing sticks. But these had been different. . . . He had seen them even before they saw him, and they had made him smile, some way—playing together in the moonlight, chasing each other like puppies, giggling fit to kill . . . Louis and Evalina used to giggle like that. But they were just babies, of course, not much older than that little white sister. Never had a chance to get any older. . . .

Tom was tired of thinking. It made his head ache. He ought to get going again, get himself to High Island while there was still time. He was just an old man, after all. What did he think he could do, anyway—fight the devil like God almighty? He had tried that when he was a lot younger and stronger, and the devil had beat him every time. What kind of chance would he have now?

He ought to go on, that was all there was to it. *Go on, you old fool,* he told himself. *Go on.*

RICHARD HAD long since given up trying to sit still. He paced up one side of the waiting room and down the other, pausing every now and again to look out the window and shake his head, or to pull his watch out of his pocket, look at it, and snap it closed. It was nearly noon, and still the storm showed no sign of abating; water was knee-deep around the train station and rising fast, while the wind was growing stronger all the time, ripping pieces of slate from the roofs of buildings and hurling them at anything or anybody that happened to be in the way. The room was crowded now with people seeking shelter. In one corner a mother tried to hush a crying baby; in another two little girls sat wide-eyed, holding a gilded bird cage between them. A small yellow bird hopped about inside it. Everywhere there were excited voices talking about the storm.

" . . . said he was down at Avenue O and Tenth—water so deep he had to swim . . ."

" . . . saw a doghouse floating with the dog on top . . ."

" . . . that woman was blown right off her porch, I'll swear . . ."

" . . . just glad I'm not in one of those houses close to the beach right now . . ."

The white-haired gentleman—Milam, the man said his name was—saw Richard flinch when he heard that. "Now, don't you worry, Mr. Carroll; I'm sure your family's just fine. . . ."

But Richard could stand it no longer. He put on his coat. "I hope you're right, Mr. Milam, but I've got to see if there's any way I can get back to them—any way atall."

"You be careful, young man. You're more good to your family alive than dead!" Mr. Milam called after him. But Richard was already out the door, wading through the rising water.

. . .

"MAMA, I cain't see nothin' but water now!" Alice hollered from her post at the window. "Water all around us!"

Mama was stirring her custard at the stove. "You'd better get away from that window, Sister. Everybody's nervous enough as it is."

"Aw, Mama, you should see it! If you just squinch up your eyes a little you'd swear we're on a big old boat!"

"You heard me, Alice."

"Yes'm," Alice said, moving away reluctantly. She sat on the floor beside Walter. He was piling up Emily's wooden blocks in stacks for her to knock down. She must have toppled fifty stacks so far, but Walter just kept piling them back up, trying not to think, trying to concentrate only on the little cubes of red and blue and yellow, the ABCs printed neatly on the sides with pictures to match—*A* for apple, *B* for bird, *C* for cat—*or catastrophe*, thought Walter. . . . *Please, God, please, make this storm stop soon.* . . .

"Walter, maybe you'd better make sure the animals are all right," Mama said. She was stirring harder than she needed to. "But come right back, you hear me? Dinner's nearly ready. I don't want you out there more than ten minutes."

"Yes, ma'am." Walter jumped up, glad to move; he was beginning to feel as if he might explode if he sat still a moment longer.

"Wait, son—put something over your head first!" his mother called to him, but he was already outside.

He wasn't prepared for the force of the wind. It had

grown so much stronger in the last few hours that it nearly blew him off his feet as he came out the door. He grabbed the stair railing to steady himself, then started down more cautiously. The two bottom steps were covered with water. Walter stepped off them and was up to his knees in brine. The big waves were still breaking to his right—off just in front of where the sand hills used to be—but their spillover was everywhere, stretching as far as the eye could see. Alice was right; the house did look like a boat. Walter remembered a time when that idea used to please him, but now it made him shiver like a dog.

He sloshed his way to the barn. Jane Long and Dowling were standing inside just where he had left them, up to their knees in salt water, too. They stared at him in mute distress. "Poor old things," he murmured, stroking their necks. "You're scared too, aren't you?"

Crockett, who had curled up on top of a bale of hay and actually managed to go to sleep, looked up and smiled a dog smile at Walter. His tail thumped in greeting.

"Hey, boy," said Walter, lifting him down, "maybe we can get Mama to let you in the house just this once." Crockett licked his face. "Come on, let's go see if the chickens are all right."

He braced himself for the wind before he stepped outside this time, then walked around the barn to the henhouse.

"Oh, no!" he cried, when he saw what had happened. The henhouse had blown over and broken to pieces. Most of the hens were dead, drowned—floating in pitiful

heaps here and there; but a few of them, along with old
Sam, were perched on top of the wreckage, looking altogether soggy and bewildered. "Oh, no," Walter repeated.
He put Crockett down; the dog's head was just above
water. "Sorry, boy," he apologized. "It's only for a minute—" Walter carried the survivors to the barn, two at a
time—even Sam Houston was too dazed to make a fuss
—and put them on Crockett's bale of hay. "You all try
not to worry, now; it's bound to be over soon," he told
the animals. Then he gave Jane Long and Dowling a
parting pat apiece and carried Crockett with him back
to the house.

"Dog!" Emily cried joyfully, when the two of them
came in, dripping salt water everywhere.

"Walter Carroll, you know that old dog isn't allowed
in the house!"

"It's just for this once, Mama—he'll drown out there!
The water's practically up to his eyeballs."

"Please let him stay, Mama!" Alice threw her arms
around the wet animal.

Their mother sniffed. "Oh, for heaven's sake, the way
you all carry on over that dog. . . . Well, I suppose he can
stay this once. But as soon as this storm's over I want him
right back outside, do you hear? Mercy, I believe I feel
a flea already!"

It was comforting, having Crockett there. He was good
as gold—never once tried to climb up on the furniture
or get into any mischief. He just sat there patiently, as if
he knew his life depended on it, letting the baby pull his
ears and poke her finger in his eye.

Walter opened his mouth to tell what had happened

to the chickens, but then he shut it again. No sense getting everybody more upset than they already were. Alice loved those old chickens; it was she who fed them and collected their eggs and cooed over the new chicks. *Lord, she practically cries every time we have fried chicken for Sunday dinner.* No, this wasn't the time to tell her. She was still remarkably cheerful, never doubting for a moment that Papa would be back soon and that everything was going to be just fine. . . .

Mama was doing her best to appear calm, to ignore the awful clamor of the storm and carry on as if nothing out of the ordinary was happening. But Walter saw her start every time a fresh blast of wind rocked the house; he heard the tightness in her voice when she spoke, smelled her fear as surely as he smelled the biscuits burning when he sat down to eat. For the first time that Walter could remember, dinner was a dismal failure. Besides the burnt biscuits, there was dry ham, gummy rice, and inedible custard. "Oh, my!" Mama cried when she tasted it. "I must've put in salt for sugar. Now, how on earth could I have done a thing like that!"

"It don't matter, Mama," Alice tried to comfort her. "We're all plenty full, anyhow."

For once Mama didn't bother to correct her grammar. She merely shook her head and began to clear away the dishes.

Just then Crockett's ears cocked up. He rose from his place under Emily's high chair and ran to the door, whining, scratching at it. . . .

Alice noticed him first. "It's Papa!" she cried, jumping up and running after the dog.

Mama's head jerked around. "Well, it's about time," she said tartly, but Walter could see relief in her face just as plain as day.

Alice was already at the door. She threw it open and flung herself into her father's arms. . . .

"Whoa, Missy!"

Lillie screamed.

Alice jumped back.

It wasn't Papa at all.

• Chapter 16

Walter stood up. "It's all right, Mama," he said. "It's just Tom. He wouldn't hurt us."

But his mother had already recovered enough to place herself protectingly between her children and the old man. She crossed her arms and faced him squarely. "What is it you want?" she shouted; with the door open she had to shout to make herself heard over the wind.

"I come to get y'all outa here!" Tom shouted back. "How come you ain't gone yet? Didn't your boy tell you what I said?"

Mama looked at Walter in confusion. "What's he talking about?"

Walter flushed guiltily. "I didn't want to scare you, Mama. He was here this mornin' when I was out doin' the milkin'—said we ought to get to higher ground. He thinks the house won't stand the storm. He's just tryin' to help us, Mama—he doesn't mean any harm. . . ."

"Help us, my eye," she muttered. "He's probably been watching the house—knows your father is away, that's all. Plannin' to rob us blind, most likely."

"No, ma'am, he ain't like that atall!"

Alice was tugging on her mother's sleeve. "Ain't you gonna let him in, Mama? Look how wet he is. He's awful old—he might die."

"He doesn't mean us any harm, Mama," Walter said again.

Tom was still standing on the doorstep, being battered by the wind and rain. In spite of her fear and suspicion, their mother wavered. Tom didn't look all that dangerous at the moment; he just looked very old and wet. Mrs. Carroll hesitated, then motioned to him. "You may come inside and close the door," she shouted.

He obeyed.

"That's far enough," she said nervously. "Alice, go get some towels—he's dripping all over the place."

Tom shook his head. "Don't worry 'bout towels, Missy. They ain't gonna do us no good today." He looked at her mother. "Ain't no time to lose. Y'all got to get outa here fast."

Mama appeared not to have heard. "I suppose you're hungry. We can fix you something to eat, let you stay in our barn till this wind and rain let up. But you'll have to go right after that. My husband won't like your being here—he's due back any minute." She said it like a warning.

Tom waved his hand impatiently. "Didn't you hear what I said? Ain't no time for food—no time to talk 'bout barns. Shoulda gone to High Island, but they ain't no time for that now, neither. If we leave right now, we might can make it to the lighthouse."

Mama stared. "The lighthouse? But that's miles from here!"

"Don't matter. I reckon it's the onliest place 'round here might still be standin' tomorrow."

Mama shuddered involuntarily. Then she got hold of herself. "Listen here, I appreciate your concern, but we'll be just fine where we are. This is a strong house; my husband built it himself. Now, as I said before, we'll be glad to feed you something, and you can stay in our barn till this storm blows over—"

"Woman, ain't you got any sense atall?" Tom exploded. "This storm ain't gonna just blow over and be gone like nothin' ever happened. This storm come straight outa hell—cain't you hear it? You think it's blowin' bad now—why, it ain't even whistlin' yet! Come dark, it's gonna knock this house down easy as spittin'. Y'all better not be inside. Maybe you don't care nothin' 'bout yourself, but you got these chirren to think of."

Emily started to cry. Mrs. Carroll walked around the table and picked her up. "I'll thank you to go, now," she said, looking proud as a queen, taller than her five feet. "You're welcome to the barn, but I won't have you in here frightening my children."

For a moment no one spoke. The wind shrieked like an unclean spirit. In his mind's eye Walter could see the dead chickens floating outside the smashed henhouse. . . .

"You won't go?" Tom said at last. "You gonna stay here and get these chirren kilt?"

"I told you to get out of my house," Mama said, her chin high. "We're not going anywhere."

Tom shook his head sadly. "Look like the devil done won again," he said, as if to himself. He stood there for another minute, shaking his head back and forth. Then he turned to go. Crockett whined and licked his hand.

Something turned over in Walter's gut. "Wait," he said, and Tom waited. Walter looked at his mother. "Mama," he said quietly, "we got to go with him."

"You hush, Walter," she said angrily. "You don't know what you're saying!"

"We got to go, Mama," he said again. "For all we know, Tom may be right. We cain't take the chance of stayin' here."

"Don't be ridiculous, Walter. You know as well as I do this storm could be over in an hour!"

"Yes'm, it could—I sure hope so—and if it is, we'll just get a little wet and come back home, that's all—no harm done. But if Tom's right, if it's just gettin' started and this house blows to pieces with us in it, we won't stand a chance."

"Walter Carroll, I won't listen to another word of this. I already said we're staying right here. You just hush— do you hear me?"

"I'm not askin', Mama. I'm tellin'. We got to go."

For a moment Mama was too astonished to speak. Alice looked at her brother wonderingly. Even Emily looked surprised somehow.

Walter had never talked back to his mother—at least, not since he was five years old and had had his mouth washed out with soap for his trouble. But he wasn't five years old anymore. For better or worse, with Papa gone, he was the man of the house.

It wasn't that he was really any more sure of himself than he had been ten minutes ago; but it had suddenly come to him, as he stood there, torn every which way inside, listening to Tom and Mama, that it didn't matter if he wasn't sure, that maybe nobody was ever really sure of anything—not even Lester Barrett, with all his swaggering—not even Papa. They all just had to do the best they could with the sense they had—maybe even believe in somebody else once in a while, the way Walter was suddenly willing to believe in Tom, right now.

"Son," said Mama, recovering her voice with an effort, "you're upset. This awful weather has us all upset—" She didn't sound angry anymore. She sounded—afraid.

"We got to go, Mama," Walter repeated gently but firmly.

Suddenly Alice threw her arms around her mother's waist. "Please, Mama," she pleaded, and her brown eyes were bright with fear for the first time all day, "I don't want to die like William—"

Mama flinched as if she had been hit. She put her hand to the black ribbon at her throat. "Nobody's going to die, Sister." For a long moment, she looked steadily at Walter, then at Tom. "All right, then," she said at last, "if we have to go, we'll go." She glanced hastily around the room. "Just let me get these dishes cleared up first. . . ."

To everyone's surprise, Tom laughed. That deep, rich laugh of his, which had sounded so out of place that night in the graveyard, seemed even stranger here, now. "Devil don't care if you done the dishes, ma'am. He's breathin' down our necks this minute. Don't do nothin' —don't take nothin' but these chirren. If we're goin', let's *go!*"

"No, sir, I'm sorry, I just can't do it. Nobody in his right mind's gonna take a boat out in water like that. It'd be the same as suicide."

Richard clenched his fists in helpless anger and walked away. The man was right—he knew it; all of the men he had spoken to had said the same thing. The bay was like something out of a nightmare—a great, gray caldron, seething with hostile waves.

But what else could he do? He had to get home; Lillie would be a wreck by now. Why, she trembled like a leaf over the least little thundershower. . . . *Poor girl*, he thought, *I guess I haven't given her much of a life . . . working hard as she does, worrying about every little thing. . . .*

Two boys splashed by, pushing bicycles. "Some storm, huh, Mister?" one of them shouted, grinning all over his fat-cheeked face—a face full of freckles, just like Walter's. . . .

Richard gritted his teeth. "You boys ought to be at home!" he shouted back. "I bet your folks are worried sick."

"It's just another overflow—nothin' to worry about!" the other boy called.

'Y'all go home—you hear me? Just go on home."

"Aw, go home yourself, Mister!" the first boy yelled over his shoulder, laughing.

"I wish I could," the frightened man muttered, as they turned the corner and disappeared. He stared out at the churning water. "Lord help me, I wish I could. . . ."

IN THE BEGINNING Tom led the way, holding Alice by the hand. Mama followed, carrying the baby; she refused to trust her to anyone else. Walter was in the rear, holding Crockett in his arms. The water was up to his thighs now. It was strangely cold for Gulf water.

"What about the other animals?" he hollered, as they neared the barn.

"Open the door!" Tom hollered back. "Nothin' else you can do for 'em now."

Alice started to cry when they came to the henhouse. "My chickens!" she wailed. "My poor chickens!"

"Don't you cry, Sister!" Mama shouted at her. "Don't you dare cry over chickens at a time like this!"

Tom tugged her along. "Your mama's right, Missy— no time to cry. You got to be brave!"

"I'm brave!" Alice glared at him through her tears.

"Good girl. You stay mad—that keep you strong, help you fight."

Mrs. Carroll stumbled and fell. The water had wound her long skirts around her legs, tripping her up. Tom and Walter helped her to her feet.

"You cain't walk in them skirts, ma'am," Tom shouted. "You got to rip 'em off!" She looked horrified.

"Please, Mama, you got to," Walter pleaded. "Here— give me the baby for a minute."

Mama saw she had no choice. Grimly, she did as she was told.

No one tried to talk much after that. Shouting wasted too much energy; they needed all of their strength just to keep moving, pushing their way through the water. Every step was a struggle, but at least the wind was mostly at their backs; it would have been impossible to go the other way—to face the blast head on. As it was, just staying together and on their feet was an almost hopeless task. Every few minutes, it seemed, one of them would trip over some unknown obstacle beneath the murky waves. But they managed, somehow, to pick themselves up again and again, to press on as best they could, while all the time, the storm was growing stronger.

IN GALVESTON at midafternoon the water was still rising. It poured into the Union Passenger Station, covering the first floor, sending all the people clambering up the stairs to the second.

"Must be a hundred or more in here, wouldn't you say, Mr. Carroll?" He and Mr. Milam were sitting on the floor, their backs pressed against a wall that shuddered as the wind assaulted it violently from the other side.

"Yes, sir, I expect so. . . ." Richard's voice was low. He had had to come back. There was nothing else he could do, no way to get home.

"Now, you mustn't be downhearted," Mr. Milam said kindly. "Trust in the Lord—that's what we have to do now. . . . Are you a religious man, Mr. Carroll?"

"Well, sir, I try to be."

Mr. Milam nodded understandingly. "I suppose that's as much as any of us can say, isn't it? Can't ask more of a man than that."

Richard didn't answer. *Maybe*, he thought, *I just haven't tried hard enough.*

There was the sudden sound of splintering glass as a piece of slate crashed through a window at the other end of the room. Several women screamed; a man had been cut on the side of the head. The crowd thronged around him. Someone shouted that he was a doctor and tried to push his way through to the injured man.

The little girls with the gilded bird cage were sitting on Richard's left now. The smaller one began to cry.

"Don't cry, Judith," the older child scolded. "You'll frighten little Bright Eyes."

"But, Anne, what if the water comes up and up and up, and Bright Eyes gets drownded!" the child wailed. She was a pretty little thing—a couple of years younger than Alice, Richard judged. He hated to see her cry so.

"That's a mighty nice bird you got there, young lady," he said.

"I know," the little girl sniffled.

"Say thank you to the gentleman, Judith," Anne reminded her.

Judith hiccupped. "Th-thank you."

"Now, what sort of bird might that be?" he asked, though he knew perfectly well it was a canary.

"A ca-n-nary."

"I see. . . . Seems to me I heard somewhere that canaries are fair singers."

"Y-yes, sir," said Judith. She blew her nose on the clean handkerchief Anne handed her. "Bright Eyes can sing p-prettier than anything!"

"Is that right? I'd sure like to hear that."

"He won't sing for you today, sir," Anne explained politely. "You see, he's a little upset with the storm and the strange place and all the people."

Richard nodded. "I can certainly understand that. I have a few birds of my own at home."

"Can they sing?" asked Judith. Her eyes were nearly dry now, her hiccups subsiding.

He chuckled. "Well, I don't know as you'd exactly call it singing," he said. "They're chickens, you see."

"Oh, chickens!" The little girls laughed. "Chickens don't sing atall," said Judith. "They just make a racket."

"Well now, don't ever let Sam Houston hear you say that! He's right proud of his voice."

"Sam Houston?" Anne looked confused. "Do you mean the famous general?"

"Oh, I imagine he considers himself a general, all right. But I don't believe he's famous just yet. This Sam Houston's our rooster."

Anne looked shocked. "You named a rooster after General Sam Houston?" She shook her head gravely. "Excuse me, sir, but that isn't seemly, is it?"

Richard smiled. "Well, no, not altogether, but I did have my reasons. You see, the real Sam Houston was a fine man—none finer, and that's a fact. But as I understand it, he was a little inclined to show off now and again—toot his own horn, so to speak. Well, that's our Sam all over."

The little girls giggled.

"Besides . . ." He lowered his voice confidentially. "I have it on good authority that the real General Sam was something of a ladies' man—married three wives, so I'm told. One at a time, naturally. Well, our Sam has him outdone on that score—he's had so many wives I've plumb lost count. We call them all Margaret, just to put a respectable face on the situation."

"Why Margaret?" asked Mr. Milam, who had been listening.

"Well, you see, the real Margaret was the third and last Mrs. Houston—the one who finally managed to tame the old boy. Why, she was so good he even mentioned her in his dying words—you ever hear that?"

No one had.

"Oh my, yes—'Texas, Margaret, Texas!' That's what he said, all right. It's written right on his tombstone for all the world to see." He winked mischievously. "It's what we say every time we have fried chicken—just as a sort of final tribute, you understand—'Texas, Margaret, Texas!' "

Anne disapproved, but Judith giggled again, and Mr. Milam laughed out loud.

There was another crash, as a second window shattered. Wind and rain poured into the room. The crowd shifted, cried out in alarm.

The children held on tightly to each other and looked up at Richard with wide eyes. "Do you think it will be over soon, sir?" Anne asked. "Our papa's out there, trying to find our big brother." There was just the barest hint of a tremble in her voice.

"Everything is going to be just fine," he said huskily. "This old storm's bound to get tired of blowing pretty soon—probably before dark, wouldn't you say, Mr. Milam?"

"Oh, I expect so, Mr. Carroll. Oh yes, certainly before dark."

Anne looked reassured. Judith peered in at the canary. "Do you hear that, Bright Eyes? Don't you be afraid—it'll be over soon." She tugged on Richard's sleeve. "Tell us another story, Mister. . . ."

We've died and gone to hell, Walter thought, *and it ain't fire and brimstone, atall—it's wind and water and water and wind . . . it's freezin' cold and raindrops that stab like knives and waves hittin' on you, washin' down your throat . . . it's bein' so tired that you'd just as soon die for the rest, but you cain't, somehow, you keep goin' and goin' and goin'. . . .*

He wondered how Tom could tell where he was leading them; Walter himself had lost all sense of direction. Everywhere he looked there was water—nothing but water. . . . Doubts slithered like snakes inside his brain —maybe Tom was turned around, maybe they were walking in circles, not getting anywhere. . . . Surely they should have passed the Buvens's house long ago, the Vaughans' . . . But then, he couldn't see much of anything through the driving rain. Every now and again salt cedar trees would loom up out of nowhere, contorted into grotesque shapes by the wind, then vanish like ghosts into the swirling gray shroud that surrounded them. . . .

Crockett had become unbelievably heavy, but Walter clung to him as if for dear life, taking comfort in his warmth, the good doggy smell of his wet fur. Besides, Mama made no complaint, though Emily must be every bit as heavy, and now Tom was carrying Alice. She had struggled mightily for as long as she could, but the water had been deeper for a good while, the swells over her head. . . .

Time seemed to have stopped altogether. Every minute was an hour, every hour an eternity. There was no yesterday or tomorrow; there was only this never-ending now, this infernal, shrieking wind and water, water and wind. . . . No way to tell how long they had been walking. . . .

Except for one inescapable fact . . . Walter was trying not to think of that. It was too awful to consider . . . but he had to consider it. It was growing darker. The light-house was still nowhere in sight, and it was growing darker. *Please, God, let us get there before it's black night. Don't leave us out here in the dark—please, God....*

Even as he prayed, the darkness deepened.

In another ten minutes, he could barely see the others moving in front of him. In twenty, they were all but invisible....

A great swell hit him, and for what seemed an eternity he was under water. His lungs felt as if they would ex-plode. Crockett struggled in his arms, and Walter let him go—maybe he would swim, be all right, somehow. . . . Walter tried to swim too, but he was tired, so tired. . . . He thought he could see William running just ahead of him, laughing over his shoulder—"You cain't catch me, Walter—see how fast I run—you cain't catch me!" Walter reached out for him, but William really was too fast for him now, too fast. . . .

At last the wave passed, and Walter was coughing up salt water, gasping for breath. He couldn't see any-thing in the darkness. The others—where were the others? He cried out frantically, but there was no an-swer. They couldn't hear him, he couldn't even hear himself over the howling of the storm . . . the storm that was the dark animal and Tom's devil and all hell rolled into one. . . .

And then he saw it. The light from the lighthouse, shining before him like a miracle—on again, off again, on again, off again. . . . And somehow William was in the light now; he had climbed up the tower steps all by himself . . . and now he *was* the light . . . But he was still so far away . . . still laughing, shouting, "You cain't catch me, Walter—you cain't catch me. . . ."

THE STORM seemed to feed on the darkness, grow fat with it, until nothing was safe from its bloated fury. Mighty waves hurled themselves over the land, smashing everything in their path. In Galveston strong brick buildings toppled as if they were made of Emily's blocks; houses, churches, steel-girdered bridges collapsed like so many matchsticks.

The crowd in the Union Passenger Station was growing more frantic by the minute. Richard had long since run out of Texas heroes to talk about, but it didn't matter; there were so many shattered windows now that the wind railing through them made it impossible to hear anyway. The little girls clung to him, Judith on his right, Anne on his left, too frightened to speak, or move, or even cry. Mr. Milam, for a wonder, was sound asleep. *There*, thought Richard, *is a man of faith.*

He himself had tried to pray, but no words would come—only pieces of pictures that tore at his heart, closed his throat—Walter's skinny arms, just beginning to flesh out a little around the muscles, Alice's pointy chin, the baby's ear, the small brown mole at the back of Lillie's neck. . . . Mutely, Richard lifted them up to heaven, as if to say, "You see, Lord—You see. . . ." It was the best he could do.

He kept expecting the train station to come thundering down around his ears any second; surely nothing made by human hands could stand such a beating much longer. The waves were leaping up so high now that their tips sprayed through the second-story windows, fifteen feet above the ground. With every wave the building lurched horribly, threatening to give way. Richard had already planned what he would do if worse came to worst—how he could take a child under each arm and try to make it to the nearest window, where they might be able to jump clear. But somehow the station kept holding together, though the storm raged on and on. . . .

It was the noise that was most unbearable, the god-awful noise of the wind. It was ten times louder than any freight train, more terrible than anything he had ever imagined. He had been through bad storms in his days at sea, heard hellish winds, but never anything like this—never, ever anything like this.

Sometime after eight o'clock there was just the hint, the barest suggestion of a lull in the wind, and a few people dared to hope, but Richard only shook his head. *It's the eye of the storm,* he told himself, and he steeled himself for the final onslaught. . . .

It came, sure enough, the mightiest wind of all. It shifted direction and blew vengefully straight out of the heart of the monster. Caught in its teeth, the iron roof of the station tore away with a hideous rumbling and roaring, showering debris on the people inside. The whole building trembled violently, as if shaken by a giant's hand. *Surely this is the end,* he thought. *May God have mercy on us all. . . .*

But an hour passed, and then another, and another, and instead of death, there came a great quiet. Slowly, almost imperceptibly at first, the wind diminished. At midnight it was no more than a strong gale. By two A.M., it had stopped altogether. In the stillness Richard could hear the sound of the waves slapping against the walls without, the sound of human sobbing within.

Mr. Milam sat up, awakened by the calm. "Well," he said, "that's better, isn't it?"

Judith looked at Richard. "Is it over, sir?" she asked.

He nodded. "It's over, sweetheart."

She sighed and buried her face in his shoulder. Her hair shone with a strange, silvery light. . . .

Vaguely it occurred to him that he could actually *see* her hair—see everything around him, in fact, more clearly than he had seen for hours and hours. . . . He looked up. Through the gash in the roof, a full moon was shining.

Bewildered by its brilliance, Bright Eyes began to sing.

BOOK THREE

The Lord on high
is mightier than the noise
of many waters, yea,
than the mighty waves of the sea.

—PSALM *93:4*

• Chapter 17

Richard Carroll opened his eyes and looked straight up into blue sky. He closed them again, confused—surely he was dreaming; the sky didn't belong inside his bedroom. . . . He would rest a few minutes more and then go hitch Dowling to the wagon. There was a load of melons he ought to get over to the Landing first thing. . . . The baby was crying. He wondered if Walter had seen to the milking yet. Emily must want her milk. . . . *Poor little Emily—don't cry, baby girl. . . . Get the baby, Alice. . . . Lillie, the baby's crying. . . .*

No. That isn't Emily. . . . Richard opened his eyes again, and this time when he saw the blue sky through the gaping hole in the station roof, he understood. He remembered. God help him, he remembered.

He had to get home. *How could I have slept even for a little while?* he wondered; *I have to get home. . . .*

Carefully, so as not to disturb the two little girls, who were still asleep, he got to his feet. One arm was numb where Judith's head had pressed against it.

"Good morning, Mr. Carroll." Mr. Milam was already

awake. All around the debris-strewn room people were moving dazedly, speaking in muted tones, some tending to the injured, some praying.

"Good morning." Richard rubbed his arm to get the circulation back in it.

"We're alive, praise the Lord."

"Praise the Lord. . . . Mr. Milam, I have to go now, find a boat, see if my family's safe—"

The old gentleman nodded. "Of course."

"These little girls—can you watch out for them, help them find their father?"

"I'll tend them as if they were my own. You go on now."

Richard put out his hand. "Good-bye, Mr. Milam."

"Good-bye, sir," he said, shaking it. "God bless you."

Richard wanted to say, "God bless you, too," but he found he could not speak. He pressed Mr. Milam's hand again, looked once more at the sleeping children, and left.

The waters had receded amazingly quickly; there was less then a foot left on the first floor of the train station. The building looked like a skeleton, with hollowed-out windows for eyes and bare bricks and beams exposed as if they were bones. But it had stood the storm. Somehow it had survived.

Richard splashed his way to the door and walked outside. Then he stopped in horror. Two dead men bobbed facedown in the water that still stood knee-deep in the street.

For a moment, he stopped breathing, as he tried to control the sickness that washed over him. Then he started to run—or run as well as he could through the wreckage that filled the street. Galveston was a shambles. Everywhere he looked there were gutted buildings, piles of rubble where buildings once stood, human bodies, carcasses of dead animals; seagulls were pecking at some of them. . . . He passed a dead horse, still harnessed to a buggy; a drowned man sat on the driver's seat, his face bloated, staring. . . .

Bewildered people were wandering the streets, looking for their families. One old woman was walking about nearly naked, crying, "Ernest! Ernest!" again and again. Richard stopped to cover her with his coat and point her toward the train station; surely someone there would be able to help her. . . . He had to get home . . . get home. . .

He made his way to the bay. The shore was littered with derelict boats and the shells of boats, and it took him some time to find one that would still float. It was just a small rowboat, but it would do. Richard thanked the owner silently, wondering if he was still alive. . . . It took him a while longer to find oars, but finally he was set, he was under way, he was on his way home.

It was a beautiful day—indecently beautiful, after what he had just seen in town. The sun shone brightly on the gently rolling water. There was a fresh little breeze blowing in off the Gulf, smelling of salt and fish. Out toward the middle of the bay, porpoises leapt and played and filled their bellies. Richard's belly was empty, but he couldn't have eaten, even if there had been anything to eat. He was sick with dread. As he traveled around the northwest tip of Galveston Island, he saw horror after horror—half-submerged hulks that yesterday had been mighty ships; others, the lucky ones, run aground, their masts twisted, broken . . . and on the shoreline, not a house standing. Not a single house.

He had to get home . . . get home. He was rowing with all his might, but it seemed to him that the boat barely moved. He maneuvered it between the jetties that protected the ship channel between Galveston and Bolivar, then turned and struck out north through the Gulf toward the middle of the peninsula.

It's a strong house, he kept telling himself, over and over. *They stood a good chance in that house, I know they did—please, God, they did. . . .*

Every muscle, every nerve strained. The sun beat down on his head, his arms, the back of his neck. He could feel its heat through his shirt, but he didn't bother to take it off, though sweat gushed from him. He had to get home . . . get home. *Good Lord in heaven, why won't this fool boat* move?

At last he could see the coast, the waves breaking up ahead on the beach. . . . *But wait!* He must have misjudged his distance somehow; this couldn't be *his* beach, *his* coast—everything looked different. . . . He must be too far to the east, or the west, or—

Lillie's palm trees. Suddenly he could see the palm trees. They were tilted at a sickening angle away from the Gulf, but they were Lillie's, all right, the palm trees that had always stood on either side of the house, two and two. . . .

Richard stopped rowing. The oars hung idle in the water; the Gulf lapped playfully at the sides of the little boat. A mullet jumped, flashing silver.

The house was gone.

. . .

FOR A MOMENT—or an hour; he couldn't have said how long—he sat in the boat, unable to move, his heart a dead weight inside his chest. Then he forced himself to go on.

The Gulf had bitten off huge chunks of the beach. The waves washed across it almost to the sand hills. Great sections of railroad track had been torn off their bed and twisted into eerie shapes that stuck up out of the surf like the claws of giant dead birds. Beyond the hills brackish water was still standing hip-deep. Here and there a fence post leaned drunkenly. The tallest of the salt grasses waved gently in the breeze. . . .

Where the house and barn had stood there was nothing but scattered boards, rubble; only the wooden blocks the house had sat upon and the steps that once led to the kitchen remained in place. For hours and hours Richard searched the debris, trying to find some trace of his family, but there was nothing, nothing. . . . The storm must have washed them out to sea. . . . He had said a thousand times that their house was the safest place there was in bad weather, strong enough to withstand any storm. And they had believed him, trusted him. Why, hadn't he built it with his own hands—his own accursed hands?

He knew it was hopeless, but still he kept searching. At length he came upon the carcasses of the cow and the mule—poor old Jane Long and Dick Dowling—but that was all. He had no tears for the unfortunate creatures; it seemed he had no tears in him at all. He was dead inside—cold and dead. He sat down on the old kitchen steps and buried his head in his hands. *Dear God,* he prayed, *if You had to take them, why did You leave me here? Where was the good in that?*

He heard no answer but the waves breaking on the new shoreline, the breeze whispering through the marsh, the laughter of the gulls. . . .

And the crowing of a rooster. It was such a familiar sound that at first Richard paid it no mind, but then it came again . . . and again . . . until finally he lifted his head and looked up. And there was Sam Houston in the low branches of one of the palm trees. *Old Sam—he made it, for a miracle. I ought to feel glad for him,* Richard thought numbly. . . . But he couldn't feel anything.

He sat there for a long time, staring up at the old rooster. Finally, he realized that it was getting darker. The sky was beginning to glow with the red of sunset. *Red sky at night, sailors delight. . . .* The words whispered in his ear, mocking him.

He couldn't stay here. He stood up. For a moment he was dizzy—light-headed with hunger and thirst and fatigue. He had had nothing to eat or drink since breakfast the day before, scarcely any sleep. But that didn't matter. Nothing mattered anymore.

He steadied himself and started walking, wading through the water. At first he turned toward High Island, but he remembered that Rollover would probably still be covered with deep water, and he was too tired to swim, too tired to go back for the boat and try to row. . . . He turned around, confused. . . .

And then he saw the lighthouse light blinking down

at Port Bolivar—on again, off again, on again, off again.
. . . *So the old lighthouse stood the storm. Well. That's
something,* he supposed. He would go there. It was as
good a place as any. He turned southwest.

A snake swam close by, sticking its ugly nose up out
of the water. Richard didn't even flinch; he didn't much
care whether it bit him or not. The snake saw him and
changed direction. Little fish darted at his feet; he
scarcely noticed them. A huge orange moon rose out
over the Gulf, just over his left shoulder. . . . Now
it was shrinking, climbing higher in the sky, fading
gradually from orange to yellow to white. . . . As he
walked, the moon followed him, spilling its light in a
shining path on the water all around him. . . .

But he never saw it.

IT WAS LONG past her usual bedtime, but Leola Sparks
couldn't sleep. From her perch at the top of the lighthouse, she looked at the moon and praised the Lord
for allowing her to see its bright face yet again. That
she owed her life to His providence, she doubted not
for a second. Unbelievers could prattle on all they
wanted about its being blind luck that had made her
decide to take the train to Galveston for her charity
work at the hospital on the very morning of the storm;
Leola knew luck had nothing to do with it. It was the
Lord, all the way—the Lord who had forced the train
to stop at Port Bolivar when the seas were too high for
the barge to cross, the Lord who had led her to take
shelter in the lighthouse, even while her own house was
smashed to splinters down at Rollover—she had seen

the wreckage through the spyglass this morning first thing—the Lord who had saved her, blessed be His Name forever and ever.

And she wasn't the only one He had saved; *why*, she thought, *there must have been more than a hundred people huddled on the lighthouse stairs while that awful wind kept blowing and blowing and the water rose higher and higher.* . . . The tower itself had swayed so badly that the machinery for the light had stopped working, and the lighthouse keeper and his wife had had to turn it by hand all through the night. But the Lord had given them the strength, and the Lord had seen to it that the lighthouse didn't fall. "He is my shield, and the horn of my salvation, my high tower, and my refuge, my saviour," Mrs. Sparks quoted aloud from second Samuel.

She stopped abruptly and peered down at the ground —or what would have been the ground if it hadn't still been covered with three feet of water. Mrs. Spark's eyes weren't what they used to be, but she thought she had seen something move. . . . *Why, yes!* There was somebody down there in the moonlight, somebody wading toward the lighthouse. *Now, who on earth?* Mrs. Sparks wondered.

"Hello! Who goes there?" she called out, her voice piercing the night with its power.

"Richard Carroll," came the faint reply.

"Did you say Richard Carroll?" Mrs. Sparks bellowed back. "Richard *W.* Carroll?"

"YES, MA'AM," he answered flatly. *Good Lord, Leola Sparks, of all people . . .*

"Heaven be praised!" cried Mrs. Sparks, and now her voice was trembling with emotion. "Here's another saved!" And then she disappeared, shrieking, into the depths of the tower.

A moment later the door at the bottom of the lighthouse flew open, and a crowd of shouting people came splashing toward him through the water. At first Richard couldn't make out who they were. . . .

And then he saw them clearly, and his heart, which he had thought was dead, nigh burst with joy.

"Papa! Papa!" Walter and Alice were crying together, as they rushed upon him and threw their arms around him.

Lillie was just behind them, carrying the baby. She tried to speak, but tears choked her; they streamed down her cheeks and shone like diamonds in the moonlight.

"Thank God," Richard managed to choke out over his own tears, as he gathered them all into his arms, "I thought I'd lost you . . . I thought . . . oh, thank God. . . ."

"Dog!" cried Emily, and Crockett leaped up to lick Richard's face, splashing water over everybody, making them all laugh—and then everyone was laughing and crying and talking all at once, the rest of the crowd, too: Audie Merle Wise and her cousin Betsy and the Langdon Huetts and Tiger Terry and a dozen or so folks from Port Bolivar and even the strangers from the train.

One old man stood apart from the rest, watching, his arms crossed over his chest, his gold tooth gleaming. Then he slipped quietly away into the shadows.

"Where's Tom?" Walter cried out all at once. "We haven't told Papa about Tom!"

"Tom?" asked Richard, confused. "Tom who?"

"Old Tom—Tom the Tramp—" a half-dozen voices answered together. "Where'd he go? He was here just a minute ago. . . ."

"He saved us, Richard," said Lillie, her eyes still brimming as she held on tightly to her husband's hand. "It was Tom that saved us. . . ."

"I swear I saw him standing right over there. . . ."

"Well, somebody go look inside the lighthouse. Maybe he went back inside. . . ."

"Tom! Where are you, Tom?"

• Chapter 18

The rescuing party came the next day and took the refugees to the Sea View Hotel in High Island, which had weathered the storm nobly.

"I wish we could just stay here forever and ever," Alice sighed happily, as she licked the last smidgeon of ice cream from her spoon for the third day in a row.

Walter shook his head. "Lord, Sister, the whole world turns upside down, and all you can think about is ice cream."

"Well, it's mighty good ice cream."

Walter had to admit that this was the truth. Food had never tasted so good; life itself had never tasted so sweet. The simple acts of eating, sleeping, even breathing—especially breathing—were pleasures beyond all imagining. . . . Sometimes, in his dreams, he was back in the wind and water, in that last terrifying hour when the dark waves were breaking over his head and he thought he would never, ever make it to the light. . . . But then something in him had refused to give up—something stubborn, hard as old Dowling's head.

. . . He couldn't have said, now, just what it was that
had sustained him; already the memory of that awful
night was becoming blurred, confused. He only knew
that somehow, somewhere, he had found the strength
to go on. He *had* made it, after all, to the light, to
safety. . . .

They had all made it, thanks to Tom. It was Tom
who had carried Alice into the lighthouse, Tom who
had gone back out into the storm for Mama and the baby,
cussing the devil all the while, fighting him tooth and
nail. And he had won. Against all odds, he had won.

But where had he gone? And *why* had he gone?
Didn't he know he was a hero? Didn't he know that
the Carroll family wanted to reward him for what he
had done? Not that they had much to reward him
with at present, but already Papa was making plans to
begin again, to plant fall crops, start work on a new
house. . . .

"Not down on our old farm," he said to Mama and
the children. "We'll settle up here in High Island,
where it's safe, and we'll have the finest farm in the
county—just you wait and see!"

Mama didn't say much, only nodded and looked at
him, her eyes full. She teared up a dozen times a day
since the storm, but her tears were different now, it
seemed to Walter. The old black ribbon was gone. It
had been washed away in the flood—torn right off her
neck—and so far, at least, she hadn't replaced it. "Maybe
it was meant to be" was all she had said.

"Mama loves Papa again, huh, Walter?" Alice whispered to her brother, who colored and shrugged her off,

wondering what age it was when girls stopped saying every single thing that came into their heads.

Mama was so subdued for the first few days after their ordeal that Walter was almost relieved to hear her arguing with Papa over the color they should paint the new house; it sounded more natural, somehow. Papa said white, like the other one; he had got used to white over the years. But Mama said she wouldn't have another white house; white was bad luck, pure and simple. Pink, now—that was a pleasant color. . . .

It was weeks before they knew fully just how fortunate they were to have survived the storm, how dreadful the loss of life had been in Galveston and on the peninsula. It was estimated that more than six thousand people had died on the island. No one was certain, because so many bodies had washed out to sea, and a large number of the ones that were recovered had to be buried quickly in mass graves. Cousin Jack Carroll and Mary Agnes were gone, and all but two of the children; by chance K. K. and Bussy had been at a friend's house in the highest part of the city and been spared.

"We'll take them in, of course," Papa said when he heard the news, and then he broke down. He had loved his old red-headed cousin.

"Of course we will," Mama said simply.

Of the small Bolivar communities, Crenshaw's, Patton, and Rollover were hardest hit. Will Strathan and his entire family were lost, all the Atkinses, the Vincents, the Blands, even old Dr. Croombs and the Barretts— every one of those big, strong brothers. . . . They said that Lester was found with his arms still locked around

Samson; he must have been trying to save the old
monster dog at the end. Walter felt sick at heart every
time he heard another name added to the list. It seemed
impossible that he'd never again hear Dr. Croombs
droning on about sin and salvation, never see Lester
at the center of a laughing crowd down at the Landing
or hear him call out, "Hey, Romeo, takin' your girl out
dancin' tonight?" Never see Fanny Kate again, either.
. . . The Vaughans had made it through the storm
miraculously by climbing to the tops of some salt cedar
trees and hanging on through the night, but now they
said they'd had a bellyful of Bolivar; they were moving
all the way to Sour Lake and never looking back.

Everything was changing. Nothing would ever be the
same again. Walter felt like an old, old man—as if he
had aged a thousand years since the summer began.
Why, he practically couldn't even remember back as far
as July; surely it was some other boy who had splashed
in the moonwater with Alice and seen Tom's campfire
glowing red down the beach—a child who dreamed of
pirates and buried treasure and hoped the old man
really was all those wild things people said he was. That
boy was gone now. Walter wasn't sure exactly where,
but he was gone, sure as shootin'. . . .

• July 1901

It was a warm evening, moonless, thick with stars. Walter had had a long day in the melon fields with his father and the new mule—Dowling the Second, they called him, as a mark of respect. After supper he decided to walk down to the beach to take in the evening air. He didn't get to the beach as often as he'd like these days. It was a longer walk than it used to be, for one thing, and then too, this had been such a busy year, what with building the new house and clearing new fields and putting in new crops. . . . A good year, all in all, for which the Carroll family could be mighty grateful, as Papa and Mama reminded the children and each other time and again—but uncommonly busy, all the same.

He walked to the water's edge. Crockett trotted along at his heels, sniffing at sand crabs. The Gulf was calm tonight. Walter wondered how he could still love it so after what he had seen it do. But he couldn't help himself. Salt water was in his blood some way, he supposed.

He sat down in the sand and stared out at the stars.

There had to be a million at least. Walter tried to count them, but he went cross-eyed after 147 and gave it up. . . .

"Hey, boy," said a voice just behind him.

For once Walter didn't holler and jump. It was almost as if he'd been expecting that voice tonight.

"Hey, Tom," he said, turning around.

It was Tom, all right. He didn't look too good—a mite more tired, more worn around the edges if that were possible. But it was the same old Tom. He put his hand down to pet Crockett, who was beside himself with joy.

"How's Missy?"

"Oh, she's just fine. We're all of us fine."

"Well, that's good. That's real good."

"Where you been, Tom? We looked for you a long time."

Tom took off his old hat and scratched his head. It must have been a new old hat—surely the other one had washed away in the storm—but it looked exactly the same. He had another shovel, too, and a gunnysack. "Oh, I been . . . 'round," he said. He grinned. "I seen y'all a time or two, when you ain't seen me."

Walter's mouth dropped open. "Is that right? Well, I'll declare, Tom, why didn't you ever stop in and say hey? We'd all have been mighty glad to see you."

"Look like that's what I'm doin' now."

"But I mean our folks'd be glad too, Tom. They've been lookin' and lookin' for you. You know, we never did get a chance to thank you properly for what you did for us. Papa nailed signs up all over, offerin' ten dollars to anybody who could help him find you. You could come live with us at our new farm—be just like part of our family."

Tom shook his head. "I ain't much of one for farmin'. Got a crawful of it a long time ago, sorta lost the appetite."

"Well, you wouldn't have to farm if you didn't want to," said Walter. "You could just live with us and go on doin' whatever you felt like—"

"Naw," said Tom. "Cain't live with walls 'round me, boy—make me feel cooped up, some way. Got to keep movin', that's all. You tell your folks I'm 'bliged, all the same."

"Aw, Tom—couldn't you come? You'd get used to the walls. It's a nice house—it really is; Papa and me built it ourselves. You could have your own room and everything. And—and, well—me and Alice, we've missed you."

The gold tooth flashed. "Oh, I'll be 'round. . . ." He leaned forward confidentially. "Course, you may not know me for the sparkle next time—liable to be a rich man by then."

"You still huntin' for treasure, Tom?"

"Got the feelin' I'm close on it, now. We done beat the devil one time, boy—you and me. He's runnin' scared these days."

They were quiet for a while. The stars grew brighter.

"I got to be goin'," Tom said at last.

"Won't you come home with me just for tonight?" asked Walter. "Have something to eat?"

Tom shook his head. "Naw, got to go. . . ." He reached into his pocket. "Got somethin' in here I been savin' for you and Missy," he said, holding the something between his thumb and index finger. It caught the starlight and gleamed palely. . . .

"The silver heart," breathed Walter. Tom put it into his hands. It was the selfsame little heart he had showed them last summer—the silver heart that had belonged to the girl from across the ocean—the heart the pirate had given her. How on earth had it survived the storm?

"But this is yours," said Walter. "We cain't take this—"

Tom shrugged. "You remember the story?"

"I remember."

"Well then, you b'long to take it, boy. I remembered a long time, but I cain't last forever. Leastways, that's what they tell me." He chuckled. "Course, I don't know—maybe I'm gonna fool 'em and be the first. . . . You take it, anyhow. Tell Missy she can wear it sometime, if she want to. Y'all pass on the story one day, 'fore you get so old you forget." He gave Crockett a parting scratch behind the ears, then started to walk away.

Crockett whined.

"Don't go, Tom," said Walter, and his voice was suddenly choked with tears that shamed him. "Please don't go."

"Got to," said Tom, grinning. "Like I say, I'll be 'round some other time. You got eyes to see, you'll see me."

THERE NEVER WAS another time. Tom died early one morning the next spring, just when the old green of the salt grass was giving way to the new, when the sun lay warm in a thousand tide pools, and laughing gulls built their nests in secret places. It was Langdon Huett who found him out on the edge of his property, over by the old Indian graveyard. He was looking for a cow of his that was due to freshen, and he found old Tom instead. Looked like he had just lain down and died easy as sleeping. His head was resting on a little pile of shells that must have marked some old grave that had been long forgotten; there were three of them, right there together, just a little way from the Indian mound. Mr. Huett had never noticed them there before, but he imagined they must have belonged to some of those old Hopkinses. A family by that name was supposed to have tried to start a sea island cotton plantation right around here way back when, but nothing had come of it. Something had killed 'em all off—yellow fever or some such. Curious, the way those shells were still piled up so neatly, after all these years. . . .

Well. Tom the Tramp. Mr. Huett scratched his head and wondered what on earth he ought to do with the poor devil. . . . Mr. Huett had been in the lighthouse when the old man had rescued Lillie Carroll and her children during that awful storm—that had been something, all right. *Who'da ever thought old Tom would turn out to be a hero?*

Mr. Huett stood there puzzling over the matter for a while. At last he breathed a sigh of relief. *I know what I'll do,* he told himself. *I'll ride over to High Island and look up Richard Carroll. He'll know what ought to be done with the old boy. Why, sure, that's what I'll do . . . just as soon as I find my cow. . . .*

. . .

THE CARROLLS buried Tom beside little William in their family plot at the High Island Cemetery. Just about everybody on the peninsula came. It occurred to Walter that Tom was far more popular dead than he ever was alive. The new preacher, name of Needham, delivered a stirring eulogy, and all the ladies cried. Afterward, Mrs. Leola Sparks sang "Abide with Me." She insisted that Tom would have wanted her to, as it had been his absolute favorite when she used to visit him in jail. She recalled how he had cried tears of joy every single time she had sung it. . . .

Walter was glad when it was all over and he had a chance to slip off by himself down to the beach. There had been a kind of dull ache in his throat all day, and nothing but the beach would soothe it.

Alice was there ahead of him. He saw her off in the distance, sitting in a miserable little heap on the sand, sobbing into Crockett's neck. Walter started to go the other way—maybe she needed to be alone for a while. But then something wouldn't let him go. He walked over and sat down beside her.

"Don't cry, Sister," he said gently, patting her shoulder. "Please don't cry."

"I c-cain't help it. All them over there singin' and talkin', and Tom just dead as a stick. . . ."

"I know, Sister, but we got to think about what the preacher said—how Tom's happy, now he's at peace—"

"How's that preacher know so much, anyhow?"

"He read it in the Bible, Sister, and you know that's the Word of God—got to be true."

Alice looked up angrily. "I don't think much of God, anyhow, lettin' ever'body die the way He does."

"Don't say that, Sister. It's bound to be a sin."

"Well, I don't care—it's the truth." Alice broke into fresh sobs. "Shoot, Walter, he never even got to find his treasure, and he looked such a l-long t-time. Seems like God could have at least let him find his treasure. . . ."

Walter struggled for the right words, but none would come. Maybe there were no words. For a long time he just sat there helplessly, patting Alice's shoulder, until at last her tears subsided, and she grew quieter.

"Walter?"

"What?"

" 'Member when we were little, how we used to talk about all the questions we were gonna ask God when we got to heaven? 'Member, I wanted to ask Him how to understand bird talk, and you wanted to ask why He ever made mosquitoes?"

Walter nodded. "Sometimes I still think if we knew that, we'd know everything."

"Maybe so. . . ." Alice wiped her nose with the back of her hand. "Well, anyway, you s'pose we could ask about Tom, too—find out the truth about who he was and everything, if that girl on the boat was really his mama and Lafitte was his papa—all of that?"

Walter shook his head. "Aw, Sister, we don't have to wait to get to heaven to find that out. We know everything we need to know 'bout Tom already."

"We do?" Alice sniffled.

"Sure we do."

"Well, who was he, then?"

Walter picked up a shell and threw it into the surf. "He was our friend," he said.

It was getting late, on toward suppertime. The sun was still up, but a lopsided moon was already rising out over the Gulf.

Alice gave one last, shuddering sigh. Crockett licked her face. "Gonna be moonwater later on," she said.

"Looks like it. . . ." Walter stood up, took her by the hand, and pulled her to her feet. The ache in his throat wasn't gone altogether, but he could stand it, now. "Come on, Sister," he said. "Let's go home."

Author's Note

Years ago, when I was a little girl growing up not far from the Texas Gulf Coast, my mother told a story that has haunted me. It was one that she had heard from *her* mother, a true story of Bolivar Peninsula, just across the water from Galveston, in the time of the Great Storm of 1900. Its hero was an old man, a tramp named Tom, who had risked his life walking miles through the rising water to rescue a family of children stranded in a house on the beach.

Two winters past, during a spell of homesickness, I began to think of writing a book with old Tom at its heart. But when I made a trip back to Texas with the intention of finding out all I could about him, I discovered that, while the actual facts of the story were certainly dramatic, they were substantially different from the tale I remembered and quite a bit briefer than I had hoped. In reality, two young sisters from Beaumont, Texas, were staying with a friend at the Patton Beach Hotel when the hurricane hit and the building had to be evacuated. One girl was swept into the waves; Tom the Tramp, who simply happened to be nearby, made his way to her and saved her life, then helped revive the other child, who had also nearly drowned. When the children's father learned what had happened, he offered Tom a job as a token of his appreciation. Later, Tom was buried in the family's plot.

That, essentially, is the whole story. As for old Tom himself, no one could tell me anything about who he really was or where he came from. This was discouraging, but elsewhere in my research I was learning all sorts of fascinating things about Bolivar and Galveston and the storm itself. Particularly compelling was the wealth of material dealing with Jean Lafitte and the rumors of buried treasure that persist even to this day. Eventually, an entirely new story with its own cast of characters began to emerge in my mind from the bits and pieces of the past I had gathered. This book is the result. Although it was inspired by an actual event, it is more the story of what might have been than of what is known for certain.

I have relied on facts whenever I could.

The history and geography of Bolivar and Galveston themselves, wherever I have mentioned them, are as accurate as I could determine from my research.

Jean Lafitte, the pirate (or privateer, as he preferred to term himself), did frequently raid slave ships and confiscate their cargo. The slaves who were brought to his Galveston Island base, Campeachy, were then sold at the price of one dollar per pound, although some of the women were kept as mistresses by the pirates.

There was a hurricane in 1818 that destroyed most of Campeachy. Afterward, because of the shortage of food

and water, it was Lafitte's decision to send all of the sur-
viving slaves to New Orleans, where they were sold at
once.

In 1844, a yellow fever epidemic in the Galveston area
took four hundred lives.

There is an Attacapa Indian burial mound near
present-day Caplen on Bolivar Peninsula. My husband
and I saw two beautiful snow-white owls not far from
there one summer night.

The National Weather Bureau forecast for the Galveston area on Saturday, September 8, 1900, as printed in
the September 7 edition of *The Galveston Daily News*,
was indeed "fair, with fresh, possibly brisk, northerly
winds on the coast. . . ." Although it had been officially
noted by the next morning that a tropical storm in the
Gulf had changed its course and was heading straight for
Texas, few Galvestonians were alarmed; they had all
seen "overflows," as they called them. As it happened, a
strong wind blowing from the north that morning did
delay the landfall of the hurricane for a time. It also
swept the bay waters over the northern part of the island
and, in clashing with the early storm tide, created what
the editor of the *Galveston Tribune* called "a magnifi-
cent spectacle" for the "student of scenery of nature."
Many went down to the beach to enjoy the show. Years
later the film director, King Vidor, who was a five-year-
old child at the time of the storm, recalled being taken
by his mother to see the waves "crash against the street-
car trestle, then shoot into the air as high as the tele-
phone poles. Higher."

Across the water that morning, on the peninsula, the
Gulf & Interstate train was attempting its usual run from

Beaumont to Galveston. It reached Port Bolivar but could go no farther, as the high seas prevented its barge crossing. Many of the train's passengers, as well as quite a few residents of the peninsula, took refuge in the lighthouse that still stands there. The lighthouse keeper and his wife, Mr. and Mrs. H. C. Claiborne, did have to turn the machinery of the light by hand to keep it operating during the storm.

At least six thousand people died that night. In Galveston two little girls named Judith and Anne Sproule escaped the rising waters, clutching a cage that held their canary.

Between eight and nine o'clock the iron roof of the Union Passenger Station was torn away. Sometime after midnight, when the storm finally passed, a full moon shone brightly on the ravaged city.

The real Tom lies buried alongside the members of the family he saved. The inscription on his tombstone reads:

TOM THE TRAMP
He alone is great
who by an act heroic
renders a real service.

But *my* Tom, and Walter, and Alice, and all the others, live only in imagination.

THERESA NELSON
Katonah, New York, 1987

Acknowledgments

The author would like to thank everyone who contributed to her research:

Mr. and Mrs. David Rogers Nelson, Jr.

Mr. and Mrs. David Rogers Nelson III

Mrs. C. A. Wise

Anne Reed Steinman Wynkoop

Jane Owens and all of the J. Frank Keith family

William and Suzanne Greene

Mrs. W. B. Fox, Jr.

Myrtis Lane

William Hardy

Jane Kenamore and the staff of Galveston's Rosenberg Library

And especially, Kevin, Michael, Brian, and Errol Cooney.

Bibliography

The following publications were most helpful:

The files of *The Beaumont Enterprise*

The files of *The Galveston Daily News*

Arthur, Stanley Clisly. *Jean Lafitte, Gentleman Rover*. New Orleans: Harmanson, 1952.

Hunter, Theresa M. *The Saga of Jean Lafitte*. San Antonio: The Naylor Company, 1940.

Lester, Paul. *The True Story of the Galveston Flood as Told by the Survivors*. Philadelphia: American Book and Bible House, 1900.

Saxon, Lyle. *Lafitte the Pirate*. New York, London: The Century Company, 1930.

And in particular:

Daniels, A. Pat. *Bolivar! Gulf Coast Peninsula*. Crystal Beach: Peninsula Press of Texas, 1985.
(with special attention to William D. Gordon's history of The Breakers).

Miller, Ray. *Galveston*. Cordovan Press, 1983.

Weems, John Edward. *A Weekend in September*. College Station and London: Texas A & M University Press, 1957.

48238821R00137

Made in the USA
Middletown, DE
13 September 2017